D0459789

Caravaggio

Signed in Blood

MARK DAVID SMITH

Caravaggio
Signed in Blood

VANCOUVER LONDON

Text © 2014 by Mark David Smith
Cover illustration © 2014 by Stéphane Jorisch
Cover design by Elisa Gutiérrez
Book design by Jacqueline Wang

Published in the UK in 2015
Published in the USA in 2016

Mixed Sources
Cert no. SW-COC-001271
© 1996 FSC
FSC
Inside pages printed on FSC certified paper using vegetable-based inks.

Printed in Canada by Sunrise Printing

2 4 6 8 10 9 7 5 3

The right of Mark David Smith to be identified as the author of this work
has been asserted by him in accordance with
the Copyright, Design and Patents Act 1988.

Cataloguing-in-Publication Data for this book
is available from The British Library.

Library and Archives Canada Cataloguing in Publication

Smith, Mark David, 1972-, author
  Caravaggio : signed in blood / Mark David Smith.

ISBN 978-1-896580-05-0 (pbk.)

  1. Caravaggio, Michelangelo Merisi da, 1573-1610--
Juvenile fiction. I. Title.

PS8637.M56523C37 2014   jC813'.6   C2014-904498-4

For Mary, my gesso;
and Miranda, Megan, and
Myles,
my ground.

—MDS

The publisher wishes to thank
Jessica Denny, Alice Fleerackers, Rachael Goddard-Rebstein,
Toni Goodall, Genie MacLeod, Verity Stone and Hannah van Dijk
for their editorial help with the book.

Tradewind Books thanks the Governments of Canada and British Columbia for
the financial support they have extended through the Canada Book Fund, Livres
Canada Books, the Canada Council for the Arts, the British Columbia Arts
Council and the British Columbia Book Publishing Tax Credit program.

 Canada Council
for the Arts
Conseil des Arts
du Canada
 BRITISH COLUMBIA
ARTS COUNCIL
Supported by the Province of British Columbia

 Canada  LIVRES CANADA BOOKS

Contents

Acknowledgements

I owe a great deal to these sources, which influenced much of my understanding of Caravaggio and his world:

M: The Man Who Became Caravaggio by Peter Robb, Henry Holt and Company, LLC, 1998.

Caravaggio: Painter of Miracles by Francine Prose, HarperCollins, 2005.

Daily Life in Renaissance Italy by Elizabeth S. Cohen and Thomas V. Cohen, Greenwood Press, 2001.

I would like to thank Mary Ann Thompson and Ian Davies, both of whom advised me on early drafts of this story; Matteo Comi, who guided my use of Italian vocabulary; and editor Lisa Ferdman, for her comprehensive revisions and her meticulous attention to detail. Finally, heartfelt thanks go to my patient substantive editor, David Stephens, and to publisher Michael Katz, who have taught me the value of precision and economy.

Chapter One: Empty Barrels and Angry Men

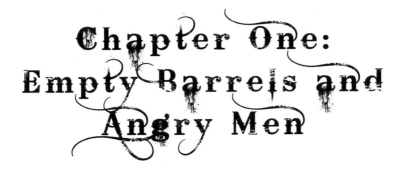

Gli uomini possono secondare la fortuna, e non opporsegli, possono tessere gli orditi, e non romperli.

Men can assist Fortune, but they cannot resist her; they may weave her webs, but they cannot break them.

~Niccolò Machiavelli

Roma, May 1606

Constantino Sparta, my bloated pig of a master and the wine seller of Piazza Navona, towered in front of me. He pointed at three stacks of oaken wine barrels in the shade of the courtyard wall. "Those," he barked, flicking his massive index finger toward the middle stack, "scrape 'em out good and send them to Signor Antonio. These," he continued, pointing to the stack on the left, "put 'em in the cellar.

And *those* over there—you leave 'em the hell alone!" He scowled. "I'm going to meet Antonio and I'll be at the *movida* till late tonight. You'd better finish your work by the time I get back, or, by *Gesù*, you'll sweat for it!"

"*Va bene*," I replied. Fine.

The wine storage room in the cellar—which also served as my sleeping quarters—had two sets of staircases leading down to it. One ran from the interior hall just behind the shop, and the other was behind a set of double doors where that fat ox was now standing.

Constantino pulled down the brim of his hat and plodded out the alley gate, his barrel-shaped torso shifting from side to side.

I feel like sticking a spigot into him.

I had already scraped one stack of junk barrels, whose oak flavour had leached out. Later, Constantino would affix new, wafer-thin oak planks to their insides to pass them off as usable. I turned to the middle stack of casks, which were going to be used for an even more knavish plan, one hatched with Signor Antonio. A bookseller to the rich, he had a shop directly across the piazza from ours. Above his premises was a printing press where he produced illegal editions of popular books. Constantino smuggled these out in his wine barrels.

The barrels were open and empty, their gaping maws pointing toward me like cannon. I picked one up and set it onto a stand. The rank air inside it was stifling—humid and close. I leaned in and pulled the two-handled drawknife toward me, slicing the old stained wood into purple curls. The fresh wood beneath looked clean, renewed. It gave me hope that things could change.

I was fifteen, and an indentured servant. After my mother's death, I might have continued living with Javier, her second husband, if he hadn't lost his ships in a storm. It was Constantino who offered to pay off the resulting debt— in exchange for my labour. In the two years that I'd been with him, all I'd learned was how to sneak and to flatter. Other boys my age were well into their apprenticeships. Me? If I stayed with this master, I'd end up either a crook and a fraud like him or a beggar on the streets.

After I had scraped the third barrel, my drawknife began to snag. Instead of making clean cuts, the blade dragged, fraying the wood's fibres. When I went to get a sharpening stone from the tool shed at the back of the courtyard, I found the door locked. *Che cavolo! What the hell! How does the old pig expect me to do the work if I can't sharpen my tools?*

Signor Antonio was meticulous about inspecting the barrels, and he'd send back any that weren't perfectly clean; he wouldn't allow them to stain his books. I couldn't very well send him half-scraped barrels—he'd be sure to give me a sound thrashing when he saw me next. "For impudence," he'd say. Then Constantino would do the same, because of the "insult" to each of their reputations. So the barrels for Signor Antonio would have to wait until my despised master returned with the key to the shed. That would save me two thrashings.

Directly above the doors to the cellar, jutting out over the second-floor window, a bar supported a hoist on a pulley. I secured ropes around the first barrel and attached a hook. Then I spat on my hands, grabbed hold of the rope and, leaning back, hoisted the barrel. It swayed as it inched upward. I let out the rope a bit at a time, until the barrel descended through the open doors to the cellar and came to rest on the floor.

I repeated this with each of the remaining barrels. For some reason, the last one felt heavier than the others. As it left the ground, it swung out of control and the rope slipped from my hands. The barrel crashed onto the top step and tipped over. Its lid popped off like a cork, and a spray of books exploded from its belly before it tumbled into the cellar. *The scoundrel is skimming books!* I scrambled down and grabbed one of the illicit editions.

El Ingenioso Hidalgo Don Quijote de la Mancha, compuesto por Miguel de Cervantes Saavedra. Spanish. I hadn't seen a Spanish book since the day Javier pulled me out of school and sold me to Constantino. *Ingenioso? Ingegnoso* in Italian. *The languages aren't so different, really.* Everybody knew a little Spanish—at least everybody at home in Sardinia. But reading it? The only thing I'd read in my two years away from home were Constantino's scribbled errand lists. *But I might be able to read this.* Pleased, I tucked the book into the back of my breeches and pulled my shirt down over it. *For later.*

I didn't think it likely that anyone would miss a single book from a whole barrel full of them. *People miscount.* But they would notice that a few were scuffed. *Che cavolo! What else can go wrong? Yet another beating!*

Just then the alley gate swung open. "Beppo! *Garzone!*" Boy!

I ran back up the cellar stairs into the courtyard.

A man in his early twenties had strolled in. He was poking at his teeth with a small metal toothpick. An older man with a black moustache and the rough chiselled face of an unfinished statue followed behind.

Ranuccio and Giovan Tomassoni were brothers who controlled the alleyways and taverns from the Ponte District to Campo Marzio. Giovan was *Capo Distrettuale*, District Head, a position of authority just below magistrate. He was always bragging in the *tavernas* about how his family had served under the Duke of Parma, fighting against the heretics.

Connections! If only I had connections.

"Where's Constantino?" Ranuccio rested one hand on the hilt of his sword and leaned into the doorway to look inside. Giovan lurked behind him.

Only two kinds of people in Roma carried swords: those who enforced the law and those who had contempt for it.

"On an errand," I answered.

"Come here, boy," Ranuccio said, crooking his finger at me.

I was afraid to approach either of them, but more afraid to say "no." So I did as he asked, glancing toward the alleyway in case I had to make a break for it.

"What's that tub of lard up to?" Ranuccio put his arm around my neck and pulled me toward him, menacingly.

"I don't know, *signore*. He never tells me anything. Maybe you could come back tomorrow and ask him."

"Tomorrow?" Giovan snorted. "Are you crazy? It's the anniversary of Pope Paul the Fifth. Tonight's the movida, then tomorrow the flotilla."

"Please, *signori*, I must return to my work."

I slipped out from under Ranuccio's arm and began to collect the spilled books.

"The wine business isn't doing so well, eh?" sniggered Giovan. He picked up one of the volumes.

"Times must be tough," remarked Ranuccio.

I couldn't think of a safe reply.

"I wonder what he's doing with Signor Antonio's books," Giovan mused aloud.

"An odd arrangement. Very odd indeed," Ranuccio added, shaking his head.

"I don't know anything about his business, signore. I just clean the barrels."

"It looks like the fat man is skimming from Signor Antonio, wouldn't you say, Ranuccio?" Giovan asked, turning the book over in his hands.

"Must be lucrative."

"I don't know anything about it!"

Without warning, Ranuccio seized a book and smashed it on the bridge of my nose. I recoiled in pain, covering my face with my hands.

"We'll return this to Signor Antonio for you," he said, waving the book in the air.

"Be sure to tell your master," called Giovan.

And they left, laughing and clapping one another on the back.

My nose didn't bleed for long but, *Dio*, was it sore! I lowered the damaged barrel into the cellar, for repair. Just as I tossed the lid in after it, the shop bell clanged.

"Beppo? Where are you?"

It was the man who lived at the home of Cardinal del Monte. His surly voice with its northern accent threw a chill up my spine. I rushed to the front of the shop. The visitor was dressed all in black, silhouetted against the sunlight like a threat. I invited him inside. His clothes were tattered and filthy, as though he slept in them and never bathed: black leggings with holes at the knees; breeches and doublet faded to charcoal. Even his beard and the thick, curly hair under his hat were dark. Only his linen shirt and collar were white. If I had not known him, I might have thought him a beggar or a traveller who had been accosted by bandits—not the most famous painter in all of Italia.

His name was Michelangelo di Merisi da Caravaggio— although he was known simply as Caravaggio, after the town of his boyhood. Those who knew him knew to avoid him.

"Signor Caravaggio, I'm sorry. I was busy out back."

"Where's your fat swine of a master, boy?"

"I don't know." I shrugged. "He's not here."

"He owes me ten *scudi* from the last painting he sold. Now, be a resourceful boy and get me the money. Actually, he owes me more than that. But I'll take the ten—unless you can find twenty. That would square his debt completely."

"Signor Caravaggio, he keeps his money on his person." I was not going to give him any of the money hidden in the wall behind the *Basket of Fruit*, the one painting still gracing the shop. "*Prego*, signore." Please. "I must get back to my work."

"Maybe, garzone, maybe—or maybe he hides it

somewhere." The painter began walking around the room, running his finger slowly along the panelling.

"Come back later, signore. Here," I cried, snatching a bottle from a straw-filled crate. "Take this wine as a gift."

He grasped it, pulled the stopper, and lifted the bottle to his lips. He had gulped half of its contents before he lowered it again.

"Constantino's wine is *merda*!" Crap! He turned the bottle upside down, spilling the wine onto the floor, and tossed the empty bottle back to me.

Then he turned and faced the painting that hid Constantino's money stash. "When he used to sell my art, *then* he had something worth buying!" His finger traced the edge of the painting—mere inches away from Constantino's purse. "Do you know how many of these damned still-lifes I used to make? Frankly, this one's rubbish compared to the others . . . still, it's worth more than twenty scudi." He placed his hands on either side of the frame, as if about to snatch it away.

"Bah! I want cash, not yesterday's fruit." He dropped his hands and turned toward the door. "I'll be back. You just make sure he has that money ready—or next time, it won't be wine I spill!"

He walked out into the sunlight, muttering under his breath.

As evening drew near, I ate a meal of stale bread and onions. Then I took my stolen book and a small oil lamp, and retired to my bed of straw in the cellar.

I found the Spanish very taxing at first, but concentrating on it helped me forget about the beating that I was sure to get. After a while, the text became easier to read. Don Quijote was some kind of low-ranking landowner who was so obsessed with romantic tales of chivalry that he had come to believe he was a wandering knight. He saw every common woman he met as a noble lady in distress. Of course, madness is funnier in stories than in real life—and more obvious too. In real life, it's often hard to tell cruelty from madness, or madness from genius.

I read late into the night. I must have fallen asleep, for I awoke to the sound of the cellar door banging open and the wooden steps groaning under a heavy weight.

"Beppo, you worthless slug!"

I rolled over. "Signore," I murmured, rubbing my eyes.

My master grabbed me by my shirt collar and dragged me upstairs. He smelled of sweat and stale wine.

"Signore, please don't!"

He pulled me through the hall and threw me onto the courtyard floor, in front of the remaining unscraped barrels.

"What are these barrels still doing here?"

"I couldn't finish scraping them because—"

"You lazy good-for-nothing!" He drove his boot into my ribs. "Antonio was expecting these. You made me look like a fool." He kicked me again.

"Aiuto!" I yelled. Help!

"I'll teach you!" Constantino shouted, shaking his fist.

The next morning, I awoke to the sound of angry voices shouting from the floor above. Bright sunlight streamed under the door at the top of the cellar stairs. My body was stiff and my head ached. As I rubbed my swollen nose, splinters of dried blood fell onto my hands, like tiny shards of red Murano glass. I got up slowly. Beneath me lay the book that I had stayed up so late to read. I tucked it into my breeches.

I crept up the stairs to the back of the shop, pausing behind a thin muslin curtain. I could see through the curtain into the shop and yet remain unseen. Oiled paper blinds covered the windows. Profiled against the yellow morning light stood Constantino, arguing heatedly with the Tomassonis.

"You'd better reconsider our offer," Giovan intoned.

Ranuccio, dressed in a bright yellow silk doublet, stood next to his brother. His left hand rested on his sword hilt.

"Twenty percent isn't much, after all," Giovan continued. "Consider it an investment in your health and well-being. If you don't cooperate, we'll tell Signor Antonio that you've been skimming."

"Blackmail! Do you thugs think you can cut in on my business? You don't know who you're dealing with!"

Ranuccio drew his sword.

"You don't scare me, you posturing brat," Constantino huffed. "Why don't you go play while the men talk?"

"You want me to play? Come play with me, fat man!" Ranuccio scoffed, carving the air with his sword.

"Are you mad?" Constantino shrieked, taking a step back. "Rani, no!"

But it was too late. Ranuccio lunged and slashed Constantino's neck.

I gasped. Blood spurted onto the wall and floor. Constantino clutched at his throat, then dropped to his knees and fell forward.

"You idiot!" Giovan hissed.

I crept back to the cellar as quickly as I could. I climbed into a barrel and tucked my knees into my chest.

The sound of boots followed me downstairs. The Tomassonis must have heard me retreating.

I pulled the barrel's lid shut just as they entered the room.

"*Nessuno*," Ranuccio said. "There's no one here."

"Maybe," Giovan replied. "Let's get out of here!"

I waited until I was sure they had gone. Then I rocked my barrel over and wriggled my way out. I was shaking as I made my way up the stairs.

The front room was quiet. I threw back the muslin curtain and stared in horror. Constantino lay dead in the middle of the floor, his limbs splayed like those of a *marionetta* whose puppet strings had been cut. Dio, there was so much blood! It was thick and almost black, like scorched oil.

I stood there transfixed, trying to figure out what to do next.

At that moment, Maria, the washerwoman, bustled through the front door of the shop with a sack of laundry. She dropped the clothes in the doorway and screamed. Then she ran out into the piazza, shouting, *"Polizia!"* Police!

Chapter Two: Run!

Solco onde, e' n rena fondo, e scrivo in vento.

I plough in water, build upon the sand, and write upon the wind.

~Francesco Petrarca

"A*spetta*, Maria!" I shouted, running after her. Wait!
But Maria had disappeared around the corner.
All at once, I remembered Constantino's stash, hidden behind Caravaggio's painting. I returned to the shop and grabbed the money, tucking it into my waistband. Then I ran out the back door, across the courtyard and into the alley.

"Alt!" a voice shouted. Stop!

Behind me, several *sbirri*, low-ranking policemen in black shirts and caps, sprinted through the courtyard.

I zigzagged up the alleys and streets, running several blocks before I burst onto the bank of the Tiber. A huge crowd was gathering for the Pope's anniversary celebration. I squeezed through the multitude, trying to shake off the sbirri.

I wound my way into an open space, where a small puppet theatre was propped up on the back of a wagon. Brave knights in miniature armour battled scowling Turks with moustaches. Every time a Turk's head fell off, the audience hooted and cheered.

I climbed up onto one of the wagon wheels and craned to see whether I was still being followed. Sure enough, half a dozen black caps were shoving their way in my direction. I leaped down and burrowed back into the crowd.

A makeshift boardwalk and ramp had been erected over the muddy flats next to the river. Musicians and jugglers cavorted around the fringes of the crowd. Amid the smaller buildings facing the riverfront stood the imposing Borghese palace.

I moved casually among the laughing and chattering onlookers. A father with his child seated on his shoulders pointed to something across the water. Two men shared a joke; one laughed so hard that he spat out the wine he was drinking. Vendors jockeyed for space: pretty young apple sellers with overflowing carts; bakers with arms full of hot loaves; hawkers calling out the prices of caged birds.

The brass emblem of a *sbirro's* cap glinted above the bystanders' heads. The policemen had split into smaller groups, in an effort to cut me off.

The spectators made way for a small troupe of performers, who stopped in front of me and erected two greased poles with iron bases.

As two strongmen tried to climb the poles, a dwarf sporting a cape and a long dangling cap taunted them and egged on the bystanders. "Come on! You call yourselves strong?" he called.

The men on the poles strained and puffed, red in the face. Veins bulged from their necks and arms. Beyond them, the caps of the sbirri closed in on me.

I grabbed the dwarf's stocking hat and pulled it onto my head. As I had hoped, it flopped down over my eyebrows. I knelt as if imitating the dwarf. The crowd laughed appreciatively. The dwarf eyed me for a moment or two, then bowed and offered me his cape. The crowd roared.

Pulling out several painted wooden balls, the dwarf proceeded to juggle them. Next, he held them out toward me and challenged, "You think you're a performer? Try juggling these!" At that moment, one of the policemen walked by. Luckily, he scanned past me.

I shuffled my hands up and down, juggling imaginary balls, as the dwarf nodded in mock encouragement. He tossed the wooden balls to me, one at a time. I held my shirt out like an apron and deftly caught them. The crowd cheered.

I did a backward somersault. The dwarf followed my lead. People laughed and began digging in their purses for small coins. The dwarf reached out to reclaim his hat, but I sidestepped him and used it to collect the *quattrini* and a few *baiocci* that came jangling into it.

"I'll take that now, and my hat," demanded the dwarf, placing a hand on a small dagger at his side. With the other, he tapped his nose. "Your friends have left."

Sure enough, the sbirri were gone.

"*Grazie*," I said, handing him his hat, his cape and the money we'd earned. Thank you.

He nodded. Winking, he flipped a small coin into my hand. Then he turned to load his props into a sack.

I pulled out Constantino's purse, added the new coin to it, and counted the money. *Thirty scudi.*

As the Pope and his entourage advanced along the river, the crowd surged toward them. The Pope was seated in splendour upon a golden throne, his white stole embroidered in gold thread with the Borghese coat of arms. Next to him, on another throne, sat his corpulent nephew, Cardinal Scipione Borghese, his thick neck spilling over the collar of his white cassock.

Chapter Three: Fatal Encounter

. . . ch'in lui non restò dramma
Che non fosse odio, rabbia, ira e furore;
Nè più indugiò, che trasse il brando fuore.

. . . in him was naught
But turned to hatred, frenzy, rage, and spite;
Nor paused he more, but bared his falchion bright.

~Ludovico Ariosto

The day was like a mad dream, its strange events piled one on top of another. The late afternoon air was heavy with the odour of moist laundry, the stench of recently slaughtered meat and the chalky smell of drying whitewash. I followed the river as it curved north, then walked several blocks east. My plan was to circle around to Piazza Navona as soon as the sbirri had abandoned their search for me. I passed blocks of brick and stone houses, some newly painted, some peeling, and some still shut after the previous night's festivities.

I stumbled into the Campo Marzio, the Field of Mars, where three boys no older than I were absorbed in a game of *morra*. Over and over again, they shouted out sums and then scooped up the money they had bet. Someone in a nightshirt burst from a doorway, holding a stick. The boys snatched their winnings and ran.

I took a shortcut down a lane that led to the Via della Pallacorda. Long ago, the street had been walled off with bricks at both ends, to form an open-air tennis court after which the street had been named. Some men were shouting, some playing, others watching from raised box seats and betting on the outcome.

The *pallacorda*, the long rope from which the game derived its name, was stretched across the street from building to building. The players ran this way and that, smacking the heavy leather ball over the rope with their racquets. I was almost halfway along the court when I realized who was playing.

Ranuccio Tomassoni. His yellow doublet lay folded over his brother's arm.

"Amateurs!" someone called out.

The players paused in their game long enough to give the speaker the evil eye.

A man dressed all in black stood mockingly at the far end of the court. "I'll show you how the game is played," he trumpeted.

Caravaggio! I've got to leave.

He grabbed the racquet from Ranuccio's hand and pushed him aside.

"I don't remember giving you permission to come around

here," snarled Ranuccio. "That is, unless you've come to pay your debts."

"Go home to mama, garzone," replied Caravaggio, "before you wet your pants."

"Perhaps you would prefer to pay in flesh," Ranuccio countered, drawing his sword.

"Pah! You think you own the streets? Step away! You're disturbing my game." The painter waved his racquet in Ranuccio's face.

"You dog's turd!" Ranuccio shrieked.

The crowd fell silent.

"Rani, let's have peace," urged Giovan, stepping over to his brother. "We can catch up with him another time."

But Ranuccio levelled his sword.

Without hesitating, Caravaggio drove a knee into his opponent's groin. Ranuccio crumpled to the ground. The painter smashed his racquet over Ranuccio's head, catching him just above the eye.

The crowd jeered.

Enraged at his brother's humiliation, Giovan unsheathed his sword and cracked the pommel over Caravaggio's head. Blood poured down one side of the painter's face. He pulled out a kerchief to cover the wound and raised his racquet to defend himself. As Giovan approached a second time, Caravaggio evaded him, parrying with his racquet.

Ranuccio picked himself up and advanced upon the painter once again.

Caravaggio's done for. Unless I can stop Ranuccio.

On impulse, I picked up the pallacorda ball—a lead pellet, wrapped in rubber, wool and leather—from where it lay on the court, and hurled it squarely into his face. *"Assassino!"* I screamed at Ranuccio. Murderer!

The ball's impact knocked him over as if he were a puppet.

"A sword!" Caravaggio shouted to the onlookers. "Get me a sword!"

"Here!" A spectator offered me his weapon. "Give us a show!"

I dashed across the court and passed the sword to Caravaggio just in time for him to fend off another swipe of Giovan's blade.

Now Caravaggio was like a cat toying with a mouse. He effortlessly parried and sidestepped each of Giovan's advances, nicking him with the tip of his sword as if he were painting: once on the calf, once on the shoulder, a dash of red here, a kiss of red there, until Giovan looked like he was fresh from a bloodletting at the barber.

Soon there were whistles and shouts in the distance. The constabulary was closing in on us.

"Andiamo!" Giovan shouted to Ranuccio, as he retreated with the crowd. Let's go!

"Come, signore!" I yelled to Caravaggio. "Polizia! Let's get away!"

Ranuccio crept up behind his enemy, sword aloft.

"Behind you!" I hollered.

Caravaggio whirled around and, as casually as if he were cutting open an envelope, slashed Ranuccio between the legs.

Everything stopped.

Everyone gawked.

Ranuccio let out a terrible scream, cupping his groin as

blood spurted through his fingers. He rolled on the ground at Caravaggio's feet.

No one should die like that, not even a thug.

Just then the police burst in, waving their truncheons and knocking the skulls of anyone in their reach.

"Run!" I tugged hard on Caravaggio's sleeve. As we fled through the throng, I couldn't resist a backward glance. Giovan was cradling Ranuccio in his arms. The wounded man lay still.

Giovan looked up at me and dragged his finger across his throat, baring his teeth like a wolf.

Chapter Four: Brief Safety

Nel tempo delle avversità si suole sperimentare la fede degli amici.

In the hour of trouble, we test the loyalty of our friends.

~Niccolò Machiavelli

Caravaggio's face was streaming with blood.

"Madama," he muttered through laboured breaths. "Casa Madama . . . del Monte! We'll be safe there."

"With the Cardinal?"

"My . . . patron. I'm under his protection."

I covered Caravaggio's head with his cape to shield him from curious eyes and draped his arm over my shoulder. He was leaning heavily on me and was breathing irregularly. I managed to half-support, half-drag him through small alleyways to the south side of Piazza Navona. At last, I pulled him into the rear courtyard of Casa Madama.

"The kitchen door," Caravaggio whispered. "It's always open."

I helped him across the broad stones of the kitchen floor and set him down on a chair. He collapsed onto the nearby table and passed out.

"Who's there?" called a middle-aged man, descending the stairway. He entered the room and gasped. "Caravaggio! Ah, Dio, what happened here?"

"He needs a surgeon."

The man lifted the handkerchief to examine Caravaggio's wound. "Who are you?" he demanded sharply.

"I'm Beppo, I'm—his servant. Please help, signore."

"Lift his legs. I'll take his arms."

I grabbed Caravaggio's legs and we carried him up a winding staircase to a long hall at the back of the house. There were seemingly endless rooms, cavernous ceiling vaults and tapestries so enormous that one could wrap elephants in them. Marble busts sat on pedestals lining the hall. Pillars rose to the ceiling. We passed a library room crammed with more books than even Signor Antonio could have seen in his entire life. Finally we came to a bedroom, where a maid was sweeping the floor. We lay Caravaggio on a high bed covered in stiff linen sheets.

"Rosa, fetch Doctor Corsilli."

"Sì, Major-domo." The young woman nodded to the chamberlain and hurried away.

"You," the major-domo said, turning to me, "wait in the hall. I'll have some food sent to you later." He pushed me out the door and rushed off down the corridor.

A servant brought me a meal on a silver tray.

"Grazie," I murmured, as she disappeared down the hall.

The covered dishes contained a sumptuous dinner: plump grapes atop thick slices of Gorgonzola cheese; a soft fresh *pane nocciato*, sourdough bread with walnuts; thin slices of chilled cooked ham, succulent and juicy; and a small ceramic cup of wine, better than any I had ever tasted. I gobbled the food greedily, leaving no crumb or drop behind.

The surgeon shuffled past, clutching his bag of instruments, and went into the bedroom.

After some time, the major-domo returned. I tried to thank him for my meal, but he rushed into Caravaggio's room. I caught a glimpse of blood-soaked bandages on the floor. The elderly surgeon was treating the gash in Caravaggio's scalp.

The door slammed shut.

Eventually, the doctor and the major-domo emerged.

"He should begin to show a bit of improvement in the next few days," the doctor stated. "He needs rest."

Not long afterward, another old gentleman entered the hall. He was tall and trim, with a salt-and-pepper beard and receding hair, a noble forehead and liquid grey eyes. He wore a green silken doublet, with delicate frills at the neck. He looked me up and down and frowned; then he turned to open the door to Caravaggio's room.

As before, I waited in the hall.

A short time later, voices spilled from the room. "And I say he shall!" Caravaggio shouted.

After a few moments, the door opened.

"Come inside," said the gentleman, beckoning to me.

As I entered, he seated himself in a plush chair near the head of the bed.

Caravaggio drew a deep breath. "Beppo, this is Cardinal del Monte."

"*Eminenza*," I said, bowing. Your Eminence.

Caravaggio closed his eyes. "No doubt this will pass, my lord. You are making too much of it."

"And you are not making enough of it," the Cardinal retorted.

"He provoked me in front of a hundred witnesses. I was merely defending myself; ask the boy."

"It matters not who provoked whom," Cardinal del Monte declared. "Ranuccio is dead."

"Yes, well, last time—"

"That was under another Pope. If you're referring to your last debacle, that was a mere assault, and the man lived to sire another child."

Caravaggio swallowed. "Ranuccio Tomassoni was no more than a hooligan. I don't see why the new Pope should care about him one way or the other."

"As you must know, the Tomassonis are a prominent family. Tensions in the north are running high."

Caravaggio shrugged. "We'll see. I've had trouble before. It's never amounted to anything."

"And this boy here"—pointing to me—"happens to be wanted for murder. You need to get rid of him."

"I didn't do it," I blurted. "Ranuccio did it! I saw him."

"What proof do you have?" the Cardinal asked, eyebrows raised.

Caravaggio sank back against the pillows. "Another

murder? What's all this about?" he queried, touching the bloodstained bandages around his head.

"This boy is wanted for the murder of his master, Constantino," the Cardinal announced. "It happened early this morning. The sbirri are looking for him everywhere."

"Too bad. That pig owed me a lot of money," Caravaggio said, dismayed.

And I have it.

Del Monte shook his head in disbelief. "You two are a fine pair. Forget the money. Do you think they will let a big fish like you slip away? The Farnese, the Borghese, and the Pamphili all side with the Spanish. Fortunately for you, I'm a Bourbon; I side with the French. We will have to get you out of here before dawn—even though the doctor says it's too early for you to be moved." He stood. "Do not even think about taking that boy with you."

The rest of the night, I sat propped up in Caravaggio's room. I nodded off a few times, but it was hardly true sleep. By the time the major-domo entered the room holding an oil lantern, my eyes felt dry and heavy.

"It's time," he barked. "Get up, boy, and help. The carriage is waiting."

The lantern's dim light cast twisted shadows across the bed. The major-domo lifted Caravaggio under the arms. He nodded to me. "Grab his legs!"

We brought the painter down the stairs and out a side door, to the stables. He winced at our every step. His breathing was shallow.

The carriage stood ready, with two fine mares and a coachman in livery. Heavy curtains concealed the interior.

We carefully laid the painter down inside. The coachman handed me a small waterskin, to give Caravaggio a drink. As I seated myself next to him, Cardinal del Monte appeared, wearing his distinctive red cassock and skullcap. At once, the major-domo cleared his throat and motioned to me to get down from the carriage. I complied, only to have Caravaggio grab me by the arm.

"No," he said. "You ride with me."

The Cardinal exploded. "You can be a fool and bring the boy if you want, but this is *my* carriage, and I'll decide who rides in it. If the boy must go along, he is to stay in the trunk."

"What about my things—my brushes, my paints?" Caravaggio protested weakly.

"You can replace them later."

The major-domo led me to a good-sized trunk at the rear of the carriage and lifted the lid. I pushed some boxes aside and settled in. He strapped down the lid. The carriage began to roll away, jostling me back and forth as it rumbled over the cobblestones.

Chapter Five:
A Miserable Journey

Chi, accecato dall' ambizione, si conduce in luogo,
dove non può più alto salir, è poi con massimo danno
di cadere necessitato.

He who, blinded by ambition, raises himself to
a position whence he cannot mount higher, must
thereafter fall with the greatest loss.

~Niccolò Machiavelli

My bones ached. I was soon doubting that it had been a good idea to come along.

As we rattled along the cobblestones, the boxes pressed into my flesh and the air in the trunk became hot and stuffy. Soon, the paving gave way to ruts of hardened earth, and my hiding place became an inferno.

We lurched along rural roads without stopping. Although I tried hard to control my bladder, the sudden jolts made this impossible. Finally I gave up trying altogether—to my shame and great relief. As if being cramped, stiff, sodden and smelling of urine weren't bad enough, the sharp turns and sudden dips in the road gave me a growing feeling of nausea, reminding me of my first storm at sea. To be seasick on land, though—surely that was a first! In time, I lost control of my stomach and began retching violently.

Then my muscles started going into spasms. I began to think that the box had been designed expressly to torture me, like an iron cage: large enough to fit into, but so small that I could barely move. I tried not to think about how much longer I would have to endure this agony.

What if I'm never able to walk again?

The pain and suffocating heat became almost unendurable. I could barely breathe. I was drenched in sweat and my throat was parched. I panicked then, believing I would die in that box. I screamed and pounded on the lid as hard as my confined limbs would allow. But it was a vain attempt, serving only to exhaust me. The clattering of the carriage and the horses' hooves must have drowned out my cries. At last, I fell unconscious. That was a small blessing.

The curse came when I woke up.

A sudden flood of light fell upon me. It was so bright that it hurt my eyes, which had grown accustomed to the trunk's darkness. A breeze heavy with the sweet smell of oleander washed over me and almost made me retch again. I was barely able to appreciate that the coach had stopped.

"Merda!" someone cried. "What a stench!"

Rough hands took hold of me, hoisting me up and sending a terrible pain through my joints and back. My limbs seemed as cramped as a dead bird's claw.

Shapes began to resolve themselves as my eyes adjusted to the light: rows of square windows and a large horseshoe-shaped courtyard with a massive portico. *A palazzo. But whose palace? Where were we?*

The main gate stood open, and beyond was a small church where the land dropped away.

I heard servants' voices.

"The master wants him brought in, but let's clean him up first."

"You clean him, then!"

"Let him clean himself!"

There were maybe a half-dozen servants, clad in simple white shirts and grey breeches.

"Speak, boy, if you can understand us."

I opened my mouth, but it could have been stuffed with peat moss for all the moisture I could find on my tongue. I blinked and swayed. Even after they drenched me with a pail of water, I was useless: mute, dizzy and paralysed.

"He's an idiot. What shall we do?"

I licked the water dripping down my face. "Water," I rasped.

"Take him to the well."

The cramping in my leg muscles gradually eased as two of the servants dragged me toward the palazzo. They gripped me tightly by the elbows, muttering under their breath. The smell of vomit and urine clung to me. Another servant followed at a distance, holding his nose.

They set me down in front of a well. The servant who had been trailing us pointed to a bucket and a cake of soap, then handed me a linen cloth, before leaving with the others.

I sat in the dirt until my numbness subsided. Eventually, I was able to fill the bucket with water and to peel off my soiled clothes. By some miracle, the book that I had tucked into the waist of my breeches was undamaged. And I still had Constantino's stash. I scrubbed my entire body vigorously. Then I wrapped the linen cloth around my waist. I washed out my shirt and breeches in the bucket and draped them over the edge of the well to dry in the hot sun.

The servants returned a short time later with the trunk in which I'd been held captive, and dropped it at my feet.

"Here. You forgot to wash this!" They walked away, hooting with laughter.

Not wishing to offend the major-domo or to be caused any more humiliation, I cleaned the trunk as thoroughly as I could, inside and out.

To my surprise, my clothes were nearly dry by the time I had finished. I dressed quickly and tried to attract the attention of a servant who rushed past. "Is signor Caravaggio—?"

"Not to be disturbed," the servant answered curtly.

"Is there anything I can have to—?"

"Kitchen," he said, pointing in its direction.

My appetite had returned, but there was no one in the kitchen and all I could find on the counter were raw vegetables and a loaf of bread. I wolfed them down. Then I went searching for my master.

I walked through a long hall filled with emblems of a noble family's wealth and power: flags and shields bearing coats of arms, burnished suits of armour and weapons mounted for display. Columns were everywhere, both real and painted. Every fresco depicted columns; even the family's coat of arms contained a column.

The staircase at the far end of the hall led to the *piano nobile*, the main floor. The residence was easily three times larger than any I'd ever been in. A throne sat at its centre. Beyond that lay a smaller room with frescoes on the walls and ceiling. One painting depicted a sea battle between armoured Christians and turbaned Turks. Flags with red crosses or with gold crescent moons waved against a backdrop of cannon fire. An assortment of galleys, both Christian and Turkish, knifed through sea swells and smoke. Despite my journey from Sardinia two years ago, I was fairly ignorant about ships—yet the scene stirred something in me. I could almost smell the sulphur of the gunpowder and hear the distant cries of wounded men.

"Do you like it?"

I turned. Caravaggio sat in the shadow of the tall curtains next to the windows.

"It's magnificent, signore."

"You think so? Hah! I would think Don Marzio could afford better artists."

The bandage around his head was loose, as if he'd tried to take it off and then to rewrap it. It looked more like a bloodied turban than a dressing. He could have been one of the Turks in the painting. He bent forward, then paused, closed his eyes, pinched the bridge of his nose and leaned back against the wall.

I walked toward him and sat down. "You are in pain, signore?"

"Sì."

"Can I help you back to your room?"

"If I wanted to be in my room, I'd be there!" he snapped.

"Of course, signore."

He took a deep breath, then indicated a portrait hanging on the adjacent wall. "The Duke of Zagarolo, Don Marzio—this is his palace. That was his father." The portrait showed a bald man dressed in battle armour, a silk ruff peeking out of the steel collar of his breastplate. "Marcantonio Colonna, the hero of Lepanto." Caravaggio put his hand on his chest in mock tribute.

"Colonna?"

"Do you know him?"

Colonna—Column. At once, I understood the reason for all the columns in the building, in paintings and on the coats of arms. The Colonnas were one of the handful of extremely powerful families—like the Borghese—who were honoured throughout Italia by the buildings, sculptures, chapels and monuments that bore their names. I did not know Marcantonio Colonna. These are not people one *knows*.

"I know who he is, of course."

"I grew up with the Colonnas. My father worked as an architect for them. They paid for my apprenticeship in Milano. The Marchesa of Caravaggio, Don Marzio's sister—she was like a mother to me." He pursed his lips and shook his head.

"I miss my mother," I blurted.

Caravaggio said nothing. His silence prompted me to go on.

"She died during childbirth."

"No brothers or sisters?"

"Brothers. But they died of the plague when I was nine.

So did my father. Do you have brothers, signore?"

"None worth speaking of."

Deciding to ignore this odd reply, I continued, "When my mother's second husband lost his ships, the creditors took everything we had. I was sent to Constantino as an indentured servant. God has blessed you, signore, to have such a family as the Colonnas to support you."

He studied me for a moment, then looked back at the fresco on the opposite wall. "Blessed? I suppose." He ground his teeth. "A kind master is a blessing to every dog. No doubt they'll give me a beautiful leash."

"I wouldn't know about that, signore. I didn't have a kind master."

"No, no you didn't. Look, Beppo, I may have made a mistake: bringing you here, I mean."

"What? Oh no, signore, no. I will help you! Whatever you need."

"Stop grovelling! I'm not sending you away. I just meant that I thought I was helping you, as you had helped me. I thought we'd come out here for a time and then go back to Roma. Instead, I find myself at their mercy."

"Signore?"

"Del Monte is making arrangements for us. It seems that we aren't staying here, and we aren't going back to Roma, either. It occurs to me that I never asked you if you wanted to come."

"That is gracious of you, signore, but I want to serve you. Only death awaits me in Roma. I'm glad to be gone from there."

I followed Caravaggio through the piano nobile back to his room in the south wing of the palazzo. He collapsed onto a high wide bed with the covers turned.

"Close the curtains," he ordered. "My head is splitting."

He turned his back to me and immediately fell asleep. I found some linens in a closet, improvised a bed on the tile floor, and fell into a deep sleep too.

I awoke when a servant opened the curtains, letting in the morning light. Caravaggio's bed was empty. The servant set a small package of clothing before me and left. I donned the garments and slipped my copy of *Don Quijote* into the breeches. I strolled out into the courtyard. My body shuddered at the sight of the major-domo's trunk, sitting next to a new carriage.

Del Monte and Caravaggio emerged from the portico, Caravaggio carrying a small wooden box under his arm.

"Well, Michelangelo, any better?" queried del Monte.

Caravaggio shrugged.

Del Monte nodded toward the box. "Don't break that. Signor Gallilei will expect it back at some point. And here." He handed Caravaggio a purse. "For the journey to Don Marzio's. I sent word ahead yesterday, so he will be expecting you." He glanced over at me. "You're taking him?"

Caravaggio nodded. "I'll be glad of his company."

As he ushered me into the carriage, I stifled a cry of relief.

A burly bearded man stepped forward and lifted his hat. The matchlock arquebuses slung over each shoulder made me nervous.

Del Monte leaned down and gave Caravaggio a fatherly kiss on the forehead. "This is Don Marzio's driver. He'll get you there in one piece."

Caravaggio sighed and closed his eyes. "Where are we headed?"

"Why, to Napoli, of course. You should be there in three days."

A look of dread crossed Caravaggio's face.

Chapter Six:
An Uncertain Road

Nessun maggior dolore
Che ricordasi del tempo felice
Nella miseria; e ciò sa il tuo dottore.

There is no greater woe
Than recollection of the happy time
In wretchedness; and this thy Sage doth know.

~Dante Alighieri

The carriage skirted the Apennine Mountains. Rocks ground under the wheels. We rolled past peasants carrying loads on their backs, and groups of impoverished men sitting around cooking fires. Every now and then, we passed a small village.

I made a few forlorn attempts at conversation, asking my new master if he was comfortable. He did not respond. Instead, he pulled his cloak over his shoulder, averted his gaze and sank deeper into his seat.

He slept most of the way.

At intervals, I chose to join the driver for company. "Have you had to use those?" I asked him, gesturing toward the arquebuses. "I mean, while driving?"

His eyes narrowed. "There's a reason I've got two of them. Wouldn't still be alive if I didn't have them both."

When we stopped at a wayside inn on the first night, I brought food up to the room I shared with Caravaggio and set it beside his bed. The next morning, I saw that the meal was untouched.

The second night, we pulled off the road and slept in the carriage.

It wasn't until the afternoon of the third day, when the carriage gave a sudden jolt, that Caravaggio erupted. His head hit the compartment's frame, and he pounded on the wall with his fist.

"Careful, *cazzone!*" he bawled at the driver. "God's bread, I could spit!" Through a gap in the curtains, he peered at the road, then turned to me. "I should be in Roma, painting for cardinals and princes!" he fumed. "Instead, I'm in a carriage headed for Napoli. Look how that idiot driver handles his matchlock! I'm surprised he hasn't shot off his foot, hauling us over these bumps."

"With respect, signore—"

"You shut up! You don't know a thing. The Tomassonis, Borghese and his fat nephew—all these stupid people now are telling *me* what to do. It's enough to drive me mad."

I sat rigidly, afraid to upset him further.

Caravaggio shook his head, slouched back into his seat and took to biting the dried skin around his thumbnail.

"And Napoli, of all the miserable places! Neapolitans—thugs and brutes, the lot of them. No appreciation for art."

I took a deep breath. "You're right. Napoli is the richest and most depraved city in the world."

The painter looked up. "Yes," he said slowly. "But how would you know?"

"I read it in a book," I replied, producing my slightly frayed copy of *Don Quijote.*

He thumbed through it. "You can read this?"

"Mostly."

"Where did you get it?"

"Constantino was smuggling them for the printer, Signor Antonio."

"Aha! And I suppose Ranuccio learned about this and killed Constantino because he wouldn't cut him into the deal? Greed and stupidity can be a fatal combination."

"Signore, when you find the time, maybe could you teach me—?"

"No apprentices. No apes following me around. I am my own master."

"I didn't mean to paint, signore. I meant to fight with a sword, like you."

He burst out laughing. It must have hurt his head to do so, because he suddenly sucked in his breath and rubbed his temples. "Teach you to fight? A scrawny whelp like you?"

"But somebody must have taught *you.*"

"Taught me? The streets of Milano taught me. Look, you want to be a fighter? Here's what you do."

I leaned forward, pleased that he had relented.

"Start with a stick, say about so big." He held his arms

apart. "You hold it like this." He placed his fists one on top of the other, holding his imaginary stick from the bottom. I imitated, nodding. "Then go find some big lout in a tavern, knock off his cap with it, and see what happens. If you survive, I guarantee you'll become a fighter—probably better than I am, ha, ha! Swords are no different."

As the carriage pitched back and forth, I leaned out the window so as to avoid smacking my head against the frame. I caught a faint whiff of smoke from the slow match, the burning end of a long hempen cord soaked in saltpetre that dangled out of the pot at the driver's side. Its orange glow proclaimed its readiness to fire the two arquebuses that he carried.

At dusk, the driver insisted that we stop at an inn. "This road is not safe at night."

I didn't like the looks of the inn. Strips of paint peeled from the walls, and some of the windows were broken.

"This place is a sty," Caravaggio declared.

"We have no choice. There isn't another inn for ten leagues."

The driver made the arrangements and led us to a room at the back, near where the horses were kept. Then he returned to the carriage to sleep. Later, a boy with matted hair and a fresh scar on his cheek brought a jug of wine and a tray of food. This time, Caravaggio ate.

He drank too. Refilling his glass, he began to recount stories of growing up in Milano and of his apprenticeship to a student of Titian's. He was always famished in those days,

Caravaggio remembered; when he first came to Roma, his studio master fed him nothing but lettuce.

Eventually, the wine, the exhaustion and the pain in his head took their toll on Caravaggio. Though unsteady myself, I bore him under the arm, downstairs and out to the backyard so he could relieve himself, before leading him back to bed.

The driver woke us before dawn. I brought Caravaggio's satchel down to the carriage just as the driver was shoving the ramrod down the barrel of an arquebus. When he set it down and picked up the second gun, I asked, "May I try?"

He shrugged and handed it to me. "Powder first, then wadding, then the lead ball, then more wadding."

I pulled the stopper off the powder horn with my teeth, and poured some of its contents into the gun barrel.

"Easy, that's enough," said the driver, watching closely.

I packed down the powder with wadding, then dropped the ball into the barrel and used the ramrod to push the ball in farther. Once I had pulled out the rod, I added a second patch of wadding, jamming the ball down even more.

"Done?"

"Not quite. Don't forget to powder the flashpan," the driver replied, grinning, "or you'll be mighty disappointed in the moment of truth!"

I added powder to the flashpan and covered it with its tight-fitting lid. "Now what?"

He took the arquebus from my hands and examined it carefully. "Now, we go, and pray that we never end up having to use this gun."

We helped Caravaggio into the carriage and rolled out onto the road in darkness. The morning light rose over the Apennines.

It wasn't until late that evening that I smelled the sea. Flat-peaked Vesuvius appeared over the plains that lay before Napoli's city wall.

I'd always thought that Roma was the *caput mundi*, the capitol of the world—but it was dwarfed by this sprawling metropolis. In Roma, three-storey buildings were common; in Napoli, towers six and seven storeys high blocked out the sun. Some of the crowded streets were barely wide enough for a cart; awnings over doorways reached across the streets and touched each other. Only in the widest streets could you be sure of the colour of the sky.

When we arrived at Don Marzio's palazzo, he was bidding farewell to a remarkably beautiful lady. A short man, with waves of grey hair that swept off his forehead, he seemed to be sailing into the wind. Despite his age, his body looked solid and powerful. If del Monte was a stag, slender and majestic, Don Marzio was a wild boar.

He kissed the lady's hand and held her gaze. She was wearing a bright silk dress and a thin veil of black lace. Her red hair flickered like a flame in the setting sun.

As her coach pulled away, Caravaggio staggered down from his carriage step as if he were a man twice his age. Servants ran to bring a chair for him.

The heat and dust of the roads had turned me into a beast of the hills—sweat soaking through my clothes.

But in his bloodied turban, my master must have felt even worse than me.

"Merisi, you've had a narrow escape," Don Marzio exclaimed. "They're scouring Roma for you. Won't be long before they realize you've fled." He nodded at me. "And the boy?"

Caravaggio looked at me and bit his lip. "I . . ." he began.

I thought his next word would be "owe" and smiled at the impending compliment. But he hesitated, then said, "He is my servant, Eccellenza."

"Very well. I received del Monte's note and, out of love for my sister, I will help you. But you're *her* pet, not mine. You can stay here until you're well enough to get about, and then you will have to find a place of your own. In the meantime, I will try to see who might be interested in offering you a commission."

"Sì, Eccellenza. You are very kind," Caravaggio replied, with a humility that I did not expect. He was quite tame in the boar's presence.

"This is an easy place to die if you anger the wrong people, Merisi. But you can also make a lot of money, if you're careful. Then you'll be able to keep a proper apprentice—if that's what you want."

"I need to get some supplies: brushes and such. I wasn't able to bring any with me."

"Your boy can get them for you. It is not safe for you to be seen on the streets."

We were given fresh clothes before being shown to a room at the south end of the palazzo. There, we found food and drink set out: breads glazed with egg white and crusted with sesame seeds, pecorino cheese studded with peppercorns, slices of fennel-scented wild pork sausage and a bowl of oranges. Still exhausted from our long journey, we ate sparingly.

Our apartment was beautifully furnished, with couches, tables, rugs and even a trundle bed for me: the first real bed I'd slept on in years.

The palazzo was in the heart of the city, across from the Santa Chiara monastery. Despite our spectacular view of the harbour, Caravaggio wanted the curtains closed.

The June heat was as harsh as the goddess after whom the month was named. The air in Napoli was suffocating at times, moist and heavy. It caused a sudden rash of pimples to break out on my face and neck. But the palace's thick stone walls and floors and the cross-breezes from the many windows kept us cool inside. I avoided leaving during the afternoon heat.

Over the next several days, I attended to Caravaggio's needs: bringing him food and drink and changing his bandages. He was weaker than when we'd left Zagarolo, and his head wound did not seem to be healing. Instead of gradually drying up, it stayed moist. After a while, I noticed a foul odour coming from the gash and asked one of Don Marzio's servants to fetch a doctor. Sure enough, the wound was festering. The doctor prescribed a poultice of strong herbs—comfrey leaves and calendula flowers in lavender oil—and wrote down the ingredients.

"You take this note to Salvatore, the apothecary up the street. If he asks, you tell him Doctor Battista needs it."

The apothecary was an old man who scuttled between endless glass jars of plants both fresh and ground, oils, powders and animal extracts. He was as bent and hunched as a shepherd's crook. He had six teeth, and the number of hairs on his shiny head was not much greater. After reading the note from the doctor, he looked up at me.

"Comfrey and calendula, eh? Someone's got a wound?"

"One of the servants," I said, quickly inventing a story. "Fell down and split his head."

"Are you one of Don Marzio's servants? Doctor Battista is Don Marzio's doctor, but I don't know you."

"I'm . . ." *No names.* "I'm new."

The apothecary gave me a gummy smile, and turned from the counter. He removed some small pale leaves and flowers that looked like deep-yellow daisies from their respective jars, and folded them into a sheet of paper. He handed them to me along with a jar of lavender oil. Then he surveyed my face and returned with something extra.

"For you: rosemary. Boil it in wine and rub it on your face and neck with a cloth. That will clean you up."

Gratefully, I offered him a coin from my purse.

"For the newest servant of Don Marzio, no charge," he said, patting my arm. "You just make sure to change that poultice four times a day."

Attending to the sleeping Caravaggio bored me almost into a trance. As much as I'd hated the tedious chores that Constantino had given me, at least they were real work; by the end of the day, I was tired. But now? *Niente*—just staring out, in a languid stupor, at the grey and yellow rooftops. Of course, I had *Don Quijote* for company, but eventually the adventures of the foolish knight with a barber's shaving bowl for a helmet seemed less amusing. All I had to look forward to was my daily visit to the apothecary, to get fresh herbs for the poultice on Caravaggio's head. Salvatore seemed to enjoy my regular visits and chattered away to me about the people he'd known, the changes he'd seen in Napoli over the years and the disrespect that the new generation had for its elders. "Not like in my day," he asserted.

After the third day, the painter's wound was noticeably less sticky, and the smell had all but gone. Within a week, a thick scab had begun to form. There probably would be a scar parting his black hair.

As his condition improved, Caravaggio ate more and slept less, but he still spoke very little. When awake, he merely stared out the window. I almost preferred his anger; at least I would have known what he was thinking.

One morning, upon my return from the apothecary, perhaps ten days after we'd arrived, I decided to try to lighten my master's mood.

"*Maestro*—" I began.

"I'm not your master," he corrected. "I told you before: I don't take apprentices."

"Of course, signore. I didn't mean it like that. But you *are* a master—a master painter. And you have been recovering for a while now, without taking a brush in your hand. Perhaps you'd like to paint again?"

"Paint what?" he growled, curling into a ball with his back toward me and pulling the sheet up over his shoulders.

"Well, something majestic," I faltered.

"There's nothing majestic outside Roma."

"Forgive me, signore. You're tired. You need rest, of course. I'll come back later."

As I turned toward the door, I noticed a folded piece of paper on the floor, next to Caravaggio's bed. I picked it up and unfolded the letter:

To His Highness, the most excellent Don Marzio Colonna, Duke of Zagarolo,

From the hand of his friend and servant, Paolo Giacommazzo, Secretary to His Most Illustrious Eminence, Cardinal Francesco Maria Borbone del Monte:

Concerning the recent events with regard to our mutual acquaintance, it is my sad duty to advise you of the trial concluded yestereve, in absentia, *which has brought a sentence of* Bando capitale. *I do not need to inform your Highness of the seriousness of this sentence, nor the risk of life this poses to him who has received it. Our friend's face is well known. In addition, His Eminence the Cardinal is concerned that the speed and urgency of the trial suggests some malevolence on the part of the judiciary. God help him if he is found.*

His companion has received the Bando di esilio *for his part in the brawl at the pallacorda. Another sentence may be forthcoming, as certain witnesses, including Giovan Francesco Tomassoni, have reported seeing Giuseppe Ghirlandi, called Beppo, fleeing the scene of Constantino Sparta's murder. As your Highness is no doubt aware—*

The door creaked open.

"Do you always read your master's letters?"

I looked up in horror. *Don Marzio.*

"Eccellenza, I . . ." I looked back at Caravaggio, hoping he would excuse my transgression, but he was silent.

"Yes?" Don Marzio inquired, leaning forward. It wasn't an invitation to speak, but rather a means of intimidation. "What does our little fugitive have to say?"

It was wisest not to answer.

"Well," he continued, "is the patient improved?"

I glanced over at Caravaggio, who remained curled up in bed, facing the wall.

"I'm not sure, Eccellenza."

"In any case, he must be moved."

"I will do whatever he needs."

"Ha!" Don Marzio snorted. "What help could you possibly be to me? You have been given the Bando di esilio— exile. Still, as long as you stay away from Roma, you're free to do whatever you like. But Merisi here has been given the Bando capitale—the death sentence, a price on his head. He is the walking dead. And the only one with the power to change that is Borghese, the Pope himself. Unless that happens—which I deem highly unlikely—all anyone needs to do to collect the reward is to cut off Merisi's head and bring it back to Roma. Since the fool has gone and painted his own cursed face into half of his paintings, no one will have any trouble recognizing him. The only part of him that will ever get back to Roma is his head—in a box! It won't be long before word gets around that Merisi is here with me. It will bring trouble right to my door. So you can't stay here any longer. I own an apartment in the Porto. You will go there tonight!"

I nodded slowly. Don Marzio already was striding out of the room.

Caravaggio mumbled something. I walked around to the other side of the bed and was surprised to find his eyes still open.

"You should have let me die in Roma," he said.

Chapter Seven:
Pain and Passion

Ahi quanto cauti gli uomini esser denno
Presso a color, che non veggon pur l'opra
Ma per entro i pensier miran col senno.

Ah! what caution must men use
With those who look not at the deed alone,
But spy into the thoughts with subtle skill.

~Dante Alighieri

The Porto apartment was less than a league from Don Marzio's palace, near the Spaccanapoli, the Napoli-splitter: the arrow-straight thoroughfare that had crossed the city since Greek times. The flat was situated on the top floor of a four-storey building set on a hill, overlooking the harbour. By the time we reached the door, Caravaggio was sweaty and out of breath.

"Too busy, here by the water, don't you agree?" I asked him. What I really meant was that, in such a crowded area, it would be nearly impossible to know who might be looking to claim the bounty on his head. "And too many stairs."

"Superb light," Caravaggio proclaimed. "It's perfect."

The next day, he gave me a list of supplies and told me where to purchase them: linen canvas and wood slats from the shipyard; chalk and walnut oil from the apothecary; lead white from the smith; pigments from the dyer; and an assortment of mirrors to be borrowed from Don Marzio— "all you can get your hands on."

"And curtains?" I questioned, reading from the list.

"For the *camera obscura*."

I gave him a blank look.

"You'll see. Just buy what's on the list and tell them to bill Don Marzio." He handed me a letter embossed with the Don's wax seal. "And add rabbit-skin glue."

Don Marzio's driver, the same one who'd brought us down from Zagarolo, came to call for me.

We drove through the city, stopping in the Mercato, the Porto and San Lorenzo. I was surprised to find that, in each neighbourhood, extremely wealthy men lived in close proximity to beggars and wretchedly poor families. And— even though it was forbidden—nearly every man, high- or low-born, wore a sword: proof that he was a fierce native Neapolitan.

I knew that I was being eyed suspiciously, and truly felt like an outsider. Still, my riding in a carriage and carrying a letter that enabled me to purchase whatever I wanted marked me as a person of status. The merchants scurried to do my bidding.

"Would the signore like to try the sable brush too? Soft as a marten's back. Perhaps a sample of something new, a yellow oxide of lead and antimony given me by an alchemist friend? Here, take it! A gift!"

Why is it that, when you are poor, no one offers you the least morsel—but when you are rich and powerful, everyone wants to give you something for free?

"The dyer had to send away for the madder red," I reported to Caravaggio when I returned. "It will take at least a week for the courier to deliver it. Oh, and the apothecary gave me this." I held out a small bag containing dried crushed leaves. "It's yarrow: 'the medicine of knights,' he called it. He said making a tea out of it will help your headaches."

Caravaggio touched his hand to his forehead. The wound had stopped festering and was closing slowly. "My headaches? What have you said?"

"Not *your* headaches, signore. I mean the headaches of the servant who fell down the stairs, the one I've been getting the poultices for every day."

He grunted, appeased. "Well, we'll see. You just keep quiet about me until I can return to Roma."

"Return? Maybe, with a pardon, you can return someday. But *I* have nothing to return to."

"For me, there is only Roma. I am sure you will find someplace you like, too."

"My place is with you," I muttered. "Without you, I'm lost."

Over the course of the summer, I learned how to stretch canvas onto bars, how to cut the ends of the wooden slats so that they locked together at right angles, how to use my feet to stretch and hold the canvas while I hammered tacks from the middle of each bar toward each corner to ensure even tension, and how to tighten the canvas by pouring hot water over it so that the fibres shrank as they dried taut as a drum. I learned how to soak and then heat the rabbit-skin glue with water and to brush the mixture—called "gesso"— onto the canvas, as a primer. I also learned how to use the mortar and pestle to grind the burnt umber, the carbon black, the yellow ochre, the lead white, the madder red and sienna into powders and to mix them with walnut oil to make paints. I even built a frame for the curtains across the middle of the room. In short, I did all the work of a painter's apprentice. Not that my master would ever call me one! By the end of July, we had many canvasses prepared and ready.

But all Caravaggio did was sit and stare at an empty chair that he'd placed in the centre of the room—or turn a sword over in his hands, watching the play of light along its edge. Days passed in this manner. Then, one late afternoon, he leaped up like a fox from a thicket and propped a canvas onto an easel, opposite the window.

"Take off your shirt," he ordered sharply.

I hesitated. But he shouted it again, so forcefully that I

complied. He had gone from melancholic to mystic; I had no idea what to expect from him next. As I removed my shirt, he retrieved the box that del Monte had given him and set it on the floor in the middle of the room. Then he adjusted the wooden screw at the back of a second easel, lowering its top bar. He picked up the box and opened it. From its blue velvet lining, he removed something clear and brilliant, the size of my fist. It was fixed in a small wooden frame.

"What is it?" I asked, astonished. "It's beautiful!"

"This? It's a lens. It *makes* beauty."

"How?"

"I'll show you."

He set it on the second easel in the middle of the room, opposite the one that held the canvas. He tightened the top bar downward, clamping the lens into place.

"Now, take this sword and stand by the window."

I walked to the window at the other end of the room. Fifteen feet in front of me was the easel with the lens, and another fifteen feet beyond that stood the easel with the canvas.

"Hold the sword with the tip down."

Caravaggio stepped over to the table and grabbed the short knife that I had used for spreading pigments. He held it between his teeth. Then he reached for a pot of the ground— the red-brown mixture of chalk, red earth and walnut oil— and brushed it hastily across the entire canvas. Setting down the brush, he took the knife from his teeth and looked at me once more before swinging the curtains shut around the lens. He barked orders from his darkened space so fast that my head started spinning.

"Hold out your arm—no, no, make a fist, tight! Tip your head back. Too much. There! Now stay still! I'm using the lens to focus your image, and I need to mark the canvas to preserve the proportions."

I looked over at the lens, but it stared back at me like an expressionless eye.

"I said: hold still!" Caravaggio thundered. "Turn your chin back. A little more. Stop."

I held my breath and body tightly.

"Nose here, chin there, elbow—that's it." After a few moments, he threw back the curtain, revealing the incisions that dotted the glossy canvas.

"Leonardo, ha! He may have written about the camera obscura, but *I'm* the one who's brought it to life!" He lay his knife back on the table. "Fine; now you are done."

Over the next week, I continued to prepare canvasses and to mix paints, occasionally modelling shirtless in front of the window. Caravaggio's headaches bothered him sometimes, but the brew of yarrow seemed to help.

One morning, a servant arrived with a message from Don Marzio.

"I have a commission," cried Caravaggio, holding the note. "Here." He tossed me a heavy pouch.

"I thought apprentices didn't get paid," I ventured.

"And *I* told you I don't keep apprentices. You're a servant. But since the commissions I get come from people with money, it is important that you look presentable in their company. That's twenty scudi. Go to Don Marzio's tailor;

he'll fix you up. And get some more madder red and walnut oil, while you're at it."

Just as with the apothecary, the tailor did not ask for payment. Instead, he said over and over again, "The Don is *molto generoso*." Very generous. I was fitted for a brocade doublet and two fine linen shirts with deep cuffs. I also was measured for leggings and pantaloons, which I was told to pick up in five days' time.

I stopped at the dyer for the madder red, then proceeded to the apothecary for the walnut oil. As the old man handed me the clay jar, he looked me straight in the eye. "Last night, bounty hunters came in looking for a painter named Caravaggio. I thought your friend with the headaches might want to know."

I nodded.

"Don't worry. Your secret is safe with me."

"Grazie, I will inform him."

We'll have to leave town. Again.

When I returned with my purchases, I found the room permeated with hot gases from a bubbling concoction of chalk, rabbit glue and lead-white mixture. Caravaggio was hard at work before two easels. One held the canvas he was painting; the other, a mirror.

"Did you get the madder red?" he asked.

"Yes, signore, but—"

"Excellent! Mix it up."

"Signore, we must leave Napoli! The apothecary said that bounty hunters came to his shop, looking for you."

My master looked up from his painting, alarmed. "Bounty hunters! When was it?"

"Last night."

He tapped his brush against the wooden palette, which was smeared with glossy lumps of brown, black, yellow and white paint. "Mix up the madder. I need to finish this." He wiped the sweat from his forehead.

I mulled the madder red in circles, smoothing it until it had the consistency of butter. All the while, I tried to work out how I could get Caravaggio to take the warning seriously. I scraped the paint into a small pot and handed it to him. He accepted it without so much as glancing at me, and scooped it onto his palette.

"God's bread, the patron wants choirs of angels and fat fluttering *putti*!" Cherubs! "You'd think the Don was testing me. Pah!"

"Signore, did you not hear me? Bounty hunters are close at hand! They mean to kill you!"

He dipped his brush into the red, and drew long streaks down the lower corner of the canvas.

"Bounty hunters, signore!" I repeated.

Caravaggio whipped around, his brush red with paint, and waved it in my face. "Do you think I've forgotten that I'm a wanted man? Here, take a look."

I gazed at the canvas, and what I saw took my breath away: Caravaggio's severed head hung from my hand, its mouth gaping in agony.

Cazzo!

"It's *David With The Head Of Goliath*," he explained. "Painting is not just my livelihood, Beppo; it's my life." He breathed deeply. "It is painting that ensures my protection and that keeps me alive. It is painting that will get me back to Roma."

"Perhaps. But I am afraid for both of us."

"*Nec spe, nec metu*—without hope or fear." He turned back to his easel, added one more touch of red, wiped the paint off the brush and set it in a pot of mineral spirits.

"There! Done."

Chapter Eight: The Courtesan's Daughter

Chi non ha danari in borsa, abbia miel in bocca.

He that has not money in his purse must have honey in his mouth.

~Italian Proverb

"**Y**ou look better," Caravaggio observed, when I returned from the tailor and donned my new attire. "It will be more seemly now for the nobles to address you."

"I'm sure they'd rather speak to you, signore."

"They can meet me later. Here's the contract for my new commission," he said, handing me an envelope. "Deliver it to the church of Pio Monte della Misericordia. When you are done, the driver will be waiting to take you to Fortunata Fiammini, the most beautiful courtesan in Napoli. She looks like Botticelli's Venus. I want you to persuade her to model for me. Tell her that Don Marzio recommended her to me, and that I would like her to portray the Virgin Mary." He adjusted a mirror on an easel.

"A courtesan will be a model for the Virgin?"

"What does it matter? I used a courtesan in Roma— Lena— for the Madonna in the chapel of the Papal Grooms. I tell you, garzone, she knew how to hold a pose. But the Cardinals ordered that the painting be taken down, two days after it was hung. It seems that too many of them recognized her!" He laughed bitterly. "*Bastardi!* But I'll get up there again. I'll have them clamouring for my work; you'll see. Instead of pulling my paintings down, they'll be using them to cover the Sistine Chapel!"

The church of Pio Monte della Misericordia had just been completed; the scaffolding was still in place. A monk met me at the entrance and led me through the building's cool interior to the sacristy, where several noblemen were waiting. They each signed the contract, while a notary witnessed their signatures. I was soon back outside in the heat. The driver was waiting for me.

A long drive through the dusty countryside brought us to Fortunata Fiammini's lavish villa, framed by manicured hedges. Statues of Apollo and Venus stood among a grove of lemon trees.

As I walked up the footpath, I practised my greeting.

"*Buongiorno, Signora* Fiammini, I am . . ." I cleared my

throat. "Signora Fiammini, it is my great pleasure to . . ."

No, that won't do.

"Allow me to escort you to Signor Caravaggio's workshop."

I paced in front of the door. "Buongiorno—no; buonGIORno, Signora Fiammini. It is an honour—"

"You have the clothes of a gentleman, but not the tongue."

I turned. A girl about my age stood in the garden. Strands of brilliant red hair peeked out from beneath her blue bonnet.

"Do you have an appointment?" she asked.

"I—I—Don Marzio sent me."

She raised an eyebrow. "Oh. Follow me." She turned toward the villa.

We passed under a portico and through an open door, into the front room. I surveyed the Turkish carpets, ceramic vases and a marble statue of a woman stepping from a bath. Floor-to-ceiling windows overlooked lush green hills. Fortunata was sitting on a divan, wearing a gold dress.

"Mother," the girl said, "Don Marzio sent this boy."

"Thank you, Dolcetta," she replied, waving the girl away.

I cleared my throat and bowed low. "BuonGIORno, Signora Fiammini. It is an honour—"

"Get to the point, young man. I'm very busy."

"My master, Caravaggio, has sent me."

"Tell him it's out of the question," she snapped.

"But, signora, he wants you to portray the Virgin Mary."

"Ha! Is he mad? Perhaps it's true what they say."

"I assure you, signora, he's perfectly sane." I caught a glimpse of Dolcetta peeking out from behind a column. She quickly ducked out of sight. "He's consumed by a passion for beauty. That's why he's a master. No other artist can match him. Soon he will be legendary—and you along with him."

"I'm sure he can find a thousand women in Napoli who are willing to sit for him."

"But none are as beautiful as you, signora! He asked me to give you this message: 'To create a masterpiece, I need a true beauty.'"

I held my breath as she tapped her lips with her finger.

Then she smiled. "Fine. Tell your master that I agree."

Fortunata and Dolcetta sat across from me in the carriage as we bounced along the road to Napoli. Occasionally, I stole glances at each of them, hoping that they wouldn't notice.

After an hour, I leaned my head out of the carriage and whistled to one of the footmen. "Prego," I said, pointing to the side of the road. "I must stop for a minute."

He shouted to the driver, who pulled over next to a low hill. One of the footmen jumped down and opened the door. The dust swirled past me as I hopped out. "I'll just be a moment," I said.

"Hurry up," the driver called, setting the wheel brake. "There are bandits everywhere."

I walked down the slope of the hill to a patch of tall grass and relieved myself. Quickly lacing up my breeches again, I scrambled back up toward the others.

"Bandits!" screamed the driver. He fumbled with the slow match and his arquebus. But before he could fire it, an arrow pierced his chest, and he fell to the ground.

I stopped in my tracks and crouched down, peering over the slope of the hill.

One of the footmen slammed the carriage door shut and raised his sword. The other bounded off the back, unsheathed his weapon, and stood beside his companion.

Three armed men ran at them. One of the assailants headed for the front of the carriage and grabbed the horses' reins, while the other two attacked the footmen, who backed up against the door. A sword nicked the carriage. The passengers screamed.

Fortunata's footmen ducked and parried the enemies' blows, until a swift kick sent one of the footmen sprawling. He slid beneath the carriage, slashing at the bandit's feet, and rolled out on the other side.

The arquebuses! I made a dash for the carriage, sprang up to the footboard and landed on the driver's bench. I grabbed one of the guns just as two more figures approached the carriage: one on horseback, the other holding a crossbow.

I placed the gunstock at my shoulder and pulled the firing string. The stock's recoil punched me hard. The bandit with the crossbow staggered back, clutching his chest, and fell to the ground. I quickly grabbed the other arquebus, attached the burning wick to the serpentine and pointed it at the apparent leader, the one on horseback.

"Call off your men!" I shouted.

"Come here!" he bellowed at them. They ran to join him on the other side of the carriage. "You could still have a life ahead of you, garzone. It's the painter I want." He rode slowly toward me.

"Not another move, if you value your life!" I shouted,

holding the firing string tight.

"Be careful," the horseman uttered menacingly, as he pulled off his hat. "Don't you recognize me?"

"Tomassoni!"

"I've come a long way, and I don't plan to leave empty-handed."

"So you attack noblewomen? You'll find no painter here. Get off your horse!" I barked at him, levelling the arquebus.

He swung himself down.

"Footman, take the reins and tie this man's horse to the back of the carriage," I commanded. Then I yanked the wheel brake and yelled to the other footman, "Get on, now!"

"Well done!" he exclaimed, jumping up beside me and taking the reins.

"Let's go!" I urged.

The horses raced off down the road. When we had covered a safe distance, I told the footman to stop. I climbed down and opened the carriage door. "Is everyone all right in here?"

"Just keep driving!" Fortunata shrieked.

I leaned in and addressed Dolcetta. "How are you faring, *signorina*?"

She didn't answer, but smiled at me until Fortunata slammed the door.

We drove the women to Fortunata's apartment in the Mercato quarter. Returning to Caravaggio, I recounted the whole tale.

"Well," he said, "you kept your wits about you. Good; you may make a fighter, after all!"

"I was lucky, signore. Sooner or later, they will find us."

"If only Tomassoni's fool of a Duke would start another war somewhere! Come, it's time for your first lesson."

We climbed the stairs to the roof. The evening sun slanted in from the west, and a light breeze blew in from the sea. The yellow roofs of Napoli spread out before us, stretching toward the blue Mediterranean.

"Spread your feet apart."

"I thought you were going to teach me to fight with a sword, signore."

"You mustn't get ahead of yourself. First lesson: balance." Caravaggio put his right foot forward and placed his left foot perpendicular to it. "Keep one foot back to act as a buttress, then bring the other forward, to lunge. Three foot-lengths should separate them."

"Like this, signore?" I copied his position.

"A little more. That's it. And turn that left foot out more. No, no, like this."

He put his own foot behind mine and pulled it toward him.

"There you go," he said. All of a sudden, he pressed his knee against mine. I collapsed and landed on my back in pain.

Kneeling next to me, my master laughed and slapped me playfully on the cheek.

"That's your second lesson: never let down your guard. That's enough for today."

Chapter Nine: Amore

Poca favilla gran fiamma seconda.

A little spark produces a great flame.

~Dante Alighieri

A dozen models, all common labourers and street hawkers, assembled at one of Don Marzio's warehouses. One woman held a small child by the hand. Caravaggio directed them to assume various poses, while I adjusted the mirrors so as to direct the light from a high window.

Fortunata and Dolcetta arrived at half-past noon.

"You're late!" the painter bawled, tossing Fortunata a burgundy gown and a shawl. "Here is your costume. You may change into it behind that screen."

"Does he always shout like that?" whispered Dolcetta.

"Yes. You'll get used to it," I replied.

When Fortunata re-emerged, Caravaggio handed the child to her and guided her to a nearby scaffold. "You are

Mary, Queen of Heaven, holding the baby Jesus. You lot, over there: resume your positions. My patrons want another typical Mary, infant Jesus and angels scene. They have no imagination. Well, we shall see."

The painter arranged the other models close together at the base of the scaffold. Two men outfitted with feathered wings perched above them, attending Mary and Jesus.

Dolcetta stole a glance at me and placed her hand on my forearm. "You were very brave on the coach."

"It was nothing," I mumbled.

She leaned in and kissed me on the cheek.

Gesù. I'm in love.

"Beppo! No more talking!" My master pointed a brush dripping with white paint at one of the women. "You, open your blouse. Everyone else: hold still."

Once Caravaggio had completed *The Seven Works of Mercy*, I rarely saw Dolcetta. I often walked past her mother's apartment in town, in hope of catching a glimpse of her. But the curtains were always drawn.

In the late afternoons, my master instructed me in the art of self-defence. He even bought me my own sword, a used but well-maintained Spanish rapier. He taught me the four positions of the hand: *prima, seconda, terza, quarta*—thumb down, in, up, out. I learned how to use imaginary circles and lines to judge distance and proportions and how to conceal a knife, protecting myself by wrapping a cape around my free arm. He also taught me how to hold my torso back and away from my attacker while keeping my sword in front of me, and how to shift my body without moving my feet.

"Begin!" he cried, standing before me with his sword at the ready.

I caught his blade on my sword's crossguard and forced it up, then turned my wrist clockwise as far as I could, and thrust. But as I did, he grabbed my sword arm and twisted it further still.

I sprawled on my back, disarmed and gasping for breath. "You're allowed to do that? To just grab my arm?"

"Allowed? We're fighting, and I'm trying to kill you, *stupido*! Forget everything you've heard about a gentleman's honour. There are only two rules in sword fighting: don't get killed, and kill your opponent. But be careful. 'All things are permissible, but not all things are profitable,' as St. Paul says. You have to know when to strike and when to wait for your attacker to make a mistake. Then you make one move: defend and attack together." He thrust his sword toward me.

I dodged just in time to avoid losing my ear—though I did lose my hat.

Caravaggio picked it up and offered it to me with a bow. We resumed our stances, circling each other, looking for an opening.

I formulated a plan of attack: *cavazione, passo grande, filo falso, riverso tondo*. Ducking my blade under his, I turned it to the outside, then took a large step forward, lifted his sword, and thrust toward him. *Perfection.* My sword point hit its mark, pressing against his shoulder. But at the same instant, I felt the pinch of his sword at my ribs.

"You can thrust at my shoulder if you wish, but I would merely be wounded; *you*, however, would be dead. Try again."

I held my sword in front of me, shielding my face, and then quickly brought it down, lunging forward. Caravaggio lifted my sword, parrying my thrust, and then tucked my blade under his arm, holding it immobile—his sword at my neck.

"You see?" He smiled. "If I get your sword, you're dead. Every move should be about creating an advantage. The edges of these blades are sharp only from the middle on. They won't hurt if you grab them farther down. Even if an edge catches you, so what? You'll have a cut on your hand, while your sword will go through your opponent's throat." He released me. "If you disable his sword, he's at your mercy. Thrust!"

I did, but he forced my sword down and pulled the pommel away from me. Now he had two swords pointed at me.

"Remove his sword and he's a dead man. Remember: strive for advantage. Now, practise what you've learned." He handed back my sword. I lifted it up and lunged into the wind.

As more patrons commissioned paintings, Fortunata began coming frequently to model, always bringing Dolcetta with her.

"Is it exciting to be apprenticed to so famous an artist?" Dolcetta asked me one day.

"I'm only his servant, not his apprentice." I leaned over and whispered, "Someday he will paint *you*."

"No," she protested. "Mother would never allow it."

"Why not?"

"That's it!" yelled Caravaggio. "You two—out!"

I motioned for Dolcetta to follow me up to the rooftop terrace.

"Is he *insane?*" she wondered aloud. "One minute he's as gentle as a lamb, and the next he's a wild beast. Why do you stay with him?"

"He has given me shelter. I'm learning a lot from him. And he needs me."

"Everyone thinks he's mad."

"Who have you spoken to about him? Don't you know our lives are in danger?"

"Truly, I haven't spoken to anyone about him. But that's what I hear." The terrace radiated heat. A muggy breeze drifted in from the shimmering sea.

"How long do you think we'll have to stay up here?" Dolcetta enquired.

"I don't know. Sometimes he paints for hours without a break."

She sighed and attempted to sit on the burning tiles. After a moment, she resolved to stand.

I pulled my copy of *Don Quijote* from my breeches, hoping to entertain her.

"You can read!" she exclaimed.

"Yes. I've been reading Cervantes. Have you heard of him? He's Spanish."

She shook her head. "Read it to me."

"Very well, my lady. Allow me to introduce you to Don

Quijote de la Mancha, the knight and protector of this castle." I bowed with a flourish, sweeping off my hat.

"Where is your armour, sir knight?"

"I am wearing it, my lady." I tapped my chest.

"And your quest, sir knight?"

"I seek the love of Dulcinea del Toboso."

"You mean Dolcetta Fiammini, don't you?"

"One and the same, my lady." I took her hand and kissed it.

"So it is *you* who are mad, not Caravaggio."

"Mad? Yes, mad for you, *señorita*." I wrapped my arm around her waist and pulled her forward, kissing her on the lips.

She returned my kiss.

"Dolcetta!" called Fortunata, appearing on the stairs.

Behind her, my master shook his head. "Beppo, you fool!"

Chapter Ten: Stolen Moments

E par che da la sua labbia si mova
Un spirito soave pien d'amore,
Che va dicendo a l'anima:—Sospira.

And from between her lips there seems to move
A soothing spirit that is full of love,
Saying forever to the soul, "O sigh!"

~Dante Alighieri

After that rooftop kiss, Fortunata thwarted my every attempt to get near Dolcetta. And whenever her mother came to model for Caravaggio, he sent me to negotiate new commissions.

The newest patron was a Genovese businessman named Giovanni Battista de'Lazzari, who wanted Caravaggio to decorate a chapel in the church of the Padri Crociferi. A painting was needed to grace the wall above the altar.

I met de'Lazzari and his notary at the church. De'Lazzari

was a pear-shaped man, thin in the face and arms, with a bulging gut.

"The work I am commissioning should depict the Holy Virgin Mary," he declared. "And angels and the infant Jesus." He swept his hands for emphasis. "And John the Baptist."

I nodded in feigned agreement. "A grand design, signore. A very grand design, indeed."

He smiled at my presumed compliment.

Grand design, my foot! This was exactly the sort of pretentious nonsense that made Caravaggio's blood boil.

"But signore, your chapel deserves a special place in the hearts and minds of its worshippers. And considering the order of nuns who serve the chapel and who care for the sick and dying, my master suggests an alternative." This wasn't quite true.

"Sì?"

"Sì. Imagine seeing your namesake, Lazarus, at the very moment that our Lord raises him from the dead. With a painting like that, your chapel will become a pilgrimage site for the sick and dying to behold Christ's power over death."

De'Lazzari nodded enthusiastically. "I like what your Master suggests. Tell him I must have a Lazarus!"

In truth, Caravaggio's concept was born more of impatience than of inspiration. When he first heard of de'Lazzari's commission, he spat out, "Tell him I'll do him a Lazarus. That's it—nothing else!"

"As to the fee—as you must know, the master receives many requests for commissions."

The notary looked back and forth between me and de'Lazzari, his pen poised above the ink pot.

"How much would he want?" de'Lazzari asked. "Eight hundred?"

I could not believe our good fortune; Caravaggio's last contract had been for four hundred scudi. "Signore, the master—"

"Fine, then! A thousand! Make it a thousand!"

If events keep unfolding like this, maybe Caravaggio will pay me enough to marry Dolcetta.

"For a thousand scudi, signore, I am sure the master will undertake your work." I bowed. *For a thousand scudi, he'd gladly paint it twice!*

Most of my time was spent in preparing Caravaggio's canvases, purchasing his colours and hiring his models. But I longed for a chance to see Dolcetta.

"When will you paint Fortunata again?" I asked my master casually.

"Who knows?" He handed me his palette and two brushes. "Clean these." He wiped his hands on a rag, then pulled out his dagger and began picking away at the flakes of paint stuck to his fingers. "Take it easy, Beppo. There's nothing you can do."

I poured mineral spirits into an empty cup and started swishing the brush around in the clear liquid until it became a chalky brown. "Can't you help me?"

"What can I do? Fortunata is not about to let her only daughter get involved with a servant."

"Dolcetta's in love with me. I *know* it."

"Yes, she does have eyes for you—not that I can see why."

"Don't tease me. I'm serious."

"Best you just let her go. I'm invited to a party tonight. I'll take you with me."

"A party? Is that safe, signore?"

"Quite safe. Only Don Marzio's people. There will be plenty of beautiful girls there."

I nodded.

I'll find a way to see Dolcetta.

Our carriage pulled up to a palazzo. Torches illuminated a stone pathway leading to a portico flanked by two pillars. A footman approached the carriage in front of us and opened the door. Fortunata stepped out.

"Forget it," Caravaggio advised me. "Dolcetta is not here. Her mother has been keeping her under lock and key lately." He smiled and clapped a friendly hand on my back. "Come on, let's have some fun."

I shook my head and sat back in my seat. "Let me take the carriage."

He sighed. "Fine. But be back by midnight. Good luck!"

Next to the gate of Fortunata's apartment was a small booth where a porter sat. I signalled the driver to stop at the gate's far corner. Then I climbed a tree whose branches hung over the wall, and jumped down into the garden. As I stood uncertainly under the balcony, Dolcetta appeared at the glass doors above.

"Beppo?" she whispered, astonished.

"Don Quijote, my Dulcinea," I teasingly corrected. "Can you come down?"

"My mother has latched my door from the outside."

"Then I'll come up."

I caught hold of two iron spindles below the railing and scrambled onto the porch. As soon as I had unlatched the doors, my beloved pulled me inside and closed them behind us.

"I had to see you."

"Hush—the servants will hear you! We haven't much time."

Before I could respond, her lips were on mine. I did not ruin the moment with words. We kissed and held each other until the church bells tolled midnight.

"Dio! I was supposed to have the carriage back by now."

"When will I see you again?"

"Can you get a message to me?"

"I will leave one with the apothecary."

We kissed once more. Dolcetta opened the glass doors, scanning the ground below for the guard.

I climbed down into the garden, scaled the wall, and jumped down next to the waiting carriage.

Chapter Eleven: Sacrilege

Aut insanit homo, aut versus facit.

The fellow's mad, or else he is composing verses.

~Quintus Horatius Flaccus (Horace)

By November, the autumn chill had made its way down to Napoli, pelting us with rain. My master had begun working in earnest on the de'Lazzari commission. One morning, as he directed the models to their places, there was a loud knock at the door. I opened it and two men entered, carrying a long wooden box.

"*Dov'è?*" queried one of them. "Where do you want it?"

"There," Caravaggio gestured, "against the wall."

A loosely wrapped corpse lay within. The linen shroud afforded a glimpse of papery grey skin. I shuddered.

"We'll be back at sundown."

"Be sure to take good care of him," the other man added, as they left. Their laughter echoed down the corridor.

"A perfect Lazarus," pronounced Caravaggio. "Now we just have to raise him up from the dead!" He pointed to two of the male models. "Pick up the body and bring it into the light."

The two remained where they were, their arms folded across their chests.

"It is not lawful," the older one declared. "You can't make me touch that."

"Cretino!" the painter burst out, plucking a dagger from his belt. "You pick him up or, by God, you'll join him in that box!"

The older man reached in quickly, trying to lift the corpse, but staggered under its weight.

"You help him!" Caravaggio ordered the younger man. Then he arranged the models: some held the corpse, while others cringed in amazement and horror.

I brought my master the paint pots and brushes as he asked for them. He kept his dagger unsheathed.

When the corpse had been retrieved, the models had left and Caravaggio had put down his brush for the evening, I confronted him. "How can you do this? It is against God's law to remove a body from its grave."

He rubbed a kerchief across the back of his neck. "Art is the only law."

My master continued to be choleric one moment and sanguine the next. It was not unusual for him to thank me and to chastise me for the very same task.

But my stolen moments with Dolcetta made everything worthwhile. Now that I knew how to gain entrance to her apartment, I slipped away to meet her at appointed times. Sometimes we talked; other times, I read to her and we play-acted parts of *Don Quijote*. This delighted her.

"Beppo," she murmured, after one of our embraces. "There is something I must tell you."

"Anything, my Lady del Toboso," I replied with a bow. I was a little unnerved by her sombre expression.

"My mother is arranging for me to be married to a nobleman's son."

A knot formed in my throat. But the creaking of the iron gate prevented me from arguing. I rushed to the window; Fortunata was returning. I had barely enough time to sneak out the window and to drop to the gravel path below. I was lucky to escape detection.

Married! What a calamity! I couldn't bear to think of Dolcetta waiting at the altar for someone else.

"Signore, *abbi pietà*!" Have mercy! A toothless old man yanked at my sleeve. He sat limply against the wall of a shop. The stench of urine rose from his clothes.

As I dug into my purse and dropped a quattrino into his cup, a figure across the street ducked into the alcove of a doorway. But it was too late; I'd seen him.

I was being followed!

I sprinted into the nearest alley, weaving past boxes and crates on my way to the harbour. Torches flickered against the walls at intervals. At last reaching the seawall, I ducked behind a loaded cart and held my breath. My pursuer whistled and waved his arms.

Two more men appeared out of the shadows.

"Is he over there?" my pursuer called out. I recognized his voice: *Tomassoni!*

"No," one of the men shouted in reply.

I was trapped between them.

The breakwater consisted of large rocks cemented together to form a steeply sloping wall. I crept over its edge and slipped into the ocean, then swam under a nearby dock.

The water was astonishingly cold.

"The noose is tightening, garzone!" Tomassoni called out. "It's only a matter of time before I have you both by the throat."

I waited until I was sure that all three were gone. Then I climbed up a piling and onto the dock. Soaked and shivering, I stumbled home.

The next morning, we headed to the Padri Crociferi to install de'Lazzari's altarpiece. "You're sure he didn't follow you?" Caravaggio asked, agitatedly. "And pull your hat down lower."

I pulled my hat down over my eyes. "I'm sure. He doesn't know where we live. We're safe for now, signore."

"No, we're not. The Pope has refused to pardon me." My master produced a parchment and waved it in the air. "My only hope now is Malta."

"Malta? It's closer to Barbary than to Roma!"

"This isn't about geography; it's about status. I've already made the necessary arrangements. Fortunata helped with some of the introductions."

I'll bet she did! To get rid of me!

"I'm going to become a knight. I'll paint there, bypass all the military nonsense and even get a title. Soon you will drop the 'signore' and call me '*Fra* Merisi.'"

The Via Nilo had become sticky with heat. We were careful to walk in the shade cast by the churches and tall apartments. Wherever we stepped from the shadows to cross a street, the sunlight seared my cheeks. I took a swig from the waterskin that I'd slung over my shoulder, then offered it to my master.

"Will I still be your servant in Malta, signore?"

"Servant?" Caravaggio drank in loud gulps. "No, you'll become my squire." He glanced over his shoulder. "Maybe I should carry your sword."

He took it before I could respond.

"Look. There's the Padri Crociferi now."

The cool and dark interior of the church was a relief from the hot sticky street. The grand entry gave way to seven flights of stairs, leading to different areas of the building. We entered the nave, walking past three of the six smaller chapels and one of the two larger ones. Paintings adorned every wall: *Our Lady, The Holy Trinity, St. Joseph and the Holy Family*. The *Lazarus* canvas was standing against a wall at the chapel's entrance. Once Caravaggio had secured a mount to the wall, I helped him to lift this latest image above the altar.

De'Lazzari soon arrived with two companions. After an exchange of greetings with the painter, there was a long moment of silence as the three men considered the work of art. They leaned in to examine the brush strokes, then stepped back to contemplate the full effect.

"Well, Signor Caravaggio," said de'Lazzari at last, "certainly it is unique."

"Unique, yes," echoed a companion. "But is this the sort of image you had in mind?"

"Too dark," asserted the other man. "A dim little chapel like this requires a painting with more colour, more light."

"You are right!" Caravaggio proclaimed. "It does not work at all!"

Before I could protest, he unsheathed the sword that he had taken from me.

"Signore, no!" I cried.

Ignoring me, he slashed the canvas from its top left corner down to the middle. Then he made a pass through its centre, leaving the painting in shreds.

De'Lazzari and his friends retreated in terror.

"Are you insane?" gasped de'Lazzari.

Caravaggio dropped the sword and stormed out a door at the far end of the chapel.

The four of us stood frozen, staring at the ruined painting.

I was the first to find my tongue. "Signori, *per favore!*" Please! "I'll be right back." I dashed through the doorway—then stopped in dismay.

Halfway up the stairs, Caravaggio sat with his head between his knees.

"Signore, what is wrong?"

He did not stir.

Just then de'Lazzari and his companions emerged from below. "Now what?" de'Lazzari demanded.

My master raised his head and glared. "I'll paint it again, and it will be even better."

I let out a deep sigh of relief.

"Three days," said Caravaggio softly. "That's all I need."
He got up and walked calmly down the staircase past his
patron, without saying a word.

I stayed behind to help remove the butchered painting.
When I arrived at our suite, my master was brushing a black
background onto a fresh canvas.

Three days later—just as promised—he was done. And even
de'Lazzari knew a masterpiece when he saw one.

Beneath a dark ceiling that occupied the painting's entire
top half, a ghastly ashen corpse was held by struggling half-
naked servants. The cadaver's left arm remained stiff, but
the power emanating from Christ's extended arm caused
Lazarus' right arm to rise in praise, so that his body formed
an unmistakable cross. Christ, the sole source of light in the
tableau, appeared to illuminate the entire room.

Every pair of eyes in the scene but one was transfixed
by Christ's miraculous power over death. At the back of the
painted crowd, unmistakable with his dark eyes and fierce
beard, stood the figure of Caravaggio himself. His hands
were clasped as though in prayer, but he was looking past
Christ into the distance beyond the picture.

At what? I wondered.

Chapter Twelve: Two Revelations

Ben perduto è conosciuto.

A thing lost, its value is known.

~Italian Proverb

Caravaggio now painted with remarkable speed. He could start and complete a grand work in the space of two weeks, without compromising his mastery. But the problem of Tomassoni remained; it was only a matter of time before he discovered where we were living.

A few weeks after my close call with Tomassoni, Don Marzio sent for me. He had an invitation for Caravaggio to a gala reception at the home of the Spanish Viceroy.

My master studied the message's ornate border. After some thought, he stated, "You shall come too, as my guest."

I couldn't hide my astonishment. "But can you trust the other guests?"

"Not at all. But since I will just have finished my latest

commission by then, I can try to move up our departure date. We can board a ship on our way back from the party. That should thwart anyone who tries to follow us. Hand me some paper!" He wrote a quick note. "Take this reply back to Don Marzio."

I tried to conceal my dismay. Accompanying my master meant leaving Dolcetta—but staying grew more dangerous by the day. And abandoning him was out of the question.

On my return journey from Don Marzio's home, I kept checking to make sure I was not being shadowed. I was worried that Caravaggio might be pressing his luck.

Later that week, we stepped out of our carriage at the Viceroy's sprawling estate west of Castel Nuovo, along the Porto. Candles flickered in clay pots along both sides of the walkway.

My heart leapt as I saw Fortunata standing ahead of us at the entrance. My master pulled me aside. "Don't get ideas, Beppo. You won't find Dolcetta at home tonight. I have that on good authority. You may as well come in and enjoy yourself. This will be your last night in Napoli."

We walked up the steps behind Don Marzio and his entourage. Caravaggio presented his invitation, which read simply, "Guest."

The herald announced, "His Highness Don Marzio Colonna, Duke of Zagarolo."

Caravaggio's entrance was not announced. Nonetheless, all eyes were upon him as we followed Don Marzio down the polished marble steps to the hall.

Women in exquisite gowns and men in ruffled silk attire held plates piled high with sumptuous cakes and dumplings and sipped wine from crystal goblets. A quartet played dance music.

"Everyone is much more elegantly dressed than we are, signore," I whispered.

"We are artists. Artists don't have to dress up."

I was ill at ease. There were too many unfamiliar faces. "Signore, this was a bad idea."

But Caravaggio reassured me. "It's all arranged; we leave tonight. No one will make a scene here and, by this time tomorrow, we'll be at sea. Now eat up! You won't see food like this for a while, I promise you!"

As he mingled with a steady stream of nobles, wealthy merchants, local officials, cardinals and bishops, my master offered a forced smile.

Finally he threw up his hands. His face stiff from the effort at strained cordiality, he muttered, "This is hell."

Just then, an elderly man with short dark hair and a long goatee drew near. "Signor Merisi. I am Juan Alfonso de Pimentel y Herrera, Viceroy to his Majesty King Philip of Spain." The Viceroy's eyes were penetrating. "With your permission, my associate wishes to speak to you." He gestured to someone standing behind us.

I was expecting another tiresome nobleman. The sight of Tomassoni made me choke.

"May I present Signor Giovan Francesco Tomassoni, a guest of his Highness the Duke of Parma? I believe you know each other already. Now, if you will excuse me, gentlemen, I will leave you to your business."

I backed away, believing that Tomassoni might throttle me.

"You remember my brother, Ranuccio, do you not?" he asked Caravaggio bluntly.

"A fine man, indeed." The painter betrayed no hint of emotion.

"I don't intend to cause any trouble here. But I assure you that, when we meet on the streets of Napoli, my brother's death will be avenged."

A door opened at the top of the staircase, and a footman commanded the crowd's attention.

"Here come the debutantes," stated Tomassoni, with an inscrutable smile. "Enjoy your evening." He turned and left.

"Ladies and gentlemen. The Spanish Viceroy is proud to present the most beautiful young women in Napoli." He paused before making the first introduction. "Signorina Fulvia Aldobrandini."

A plump young lady dressed in shimmering silks made her entrance. She held the hem of her gown in one hand and clasped her escort's arm with the other. When they had descended the stairs and had reached the hall, they were introduced to the group of young men gathered around Tomassoni. Each young man ceremoniously kissed the girl's hand.

"Signorina Isabella Orsini."

A short girl in an oversized ball gown made her way down the staircase on the arm of a slender man.

"Signorina Francesca Giustiniani."

"This one is beautiful, is she not?" Caravaggio remarked.

I shrugged. "Not as beautiful as my Dolcetta."

"Signorina Dolcetta Fiammini," the herald announced.

I shot Caravaggio a look.

"Don't say I didn't warn you, Beppo. You're not in her league."

Dolcetta wore a spectacular scarlet-and-gold gown. Her red hair was tied in a knot at the back of her neck. She hesitated for a moment at the top of the stairs. Don Marzio offered his arm, and she placed her gloved hand on top of it. Then she descended and proceeded toward the group of young men. Tomassoni was the first to step forward to kiss her hand. He cast a glance in my direction, grinning smugly.

Once all of the debutantes had been introduced, I tried to approach Dolcetta. She was standing in the middle of the room with the other young women. They were joined by the young noblemen, who selected partners from amongst them. All the couples instantly were swept up into a *pavan*. Dolcetta floated past me in Tomassoni's arms. I ached at her grace.

I longed to jump Tomassoni, but Caravaggio grabbed me and dragged me aside. "Don't be a fool. We have bigger problems to contend with." He nodded toward several dark figures standing together at the door. *Tomassoni's men.*

I slumped back against a column.

Despite my efforts all evening long, I could not catch Dolcetta's eye. She kept her gaze steadily focused on her dance partners. As the ball drew to a close, she left without even a glance in my direction.

"We must leave," Caravaggio said urgently, firmly clamping his hand onto my shoulder. He quickly led me down the servants' corridor.

Our carriage rolled out the rear gate onto an empty street. The music of the party dissolved behind us.

"Don't worry, garzone. Another week and you'll have forgotten all about her."

I flew into a rage. "What do *you* know about it? I have to talk to her!" I flung open the carriage door and jumped into the street.

"Wait!" yelled Caravaggio.

Napoli is raucous at night. The daytime peal of church bells and the call of the fruit-seller are replaced by laughter and cursing, music and the barking of dogs. I raced toward Dolcetta's apartment through dimly lit streets peopled with drunks and vagabonds.

I scaled the wall of her building, making sure to keep out of the guard's sight, and tossed a pebble against her bedroom window. My beloved appeared on the balcony. "Who's there?" she called.

"It's me. Beppo."

"Beppo!" Her voice dropped to a whisper. "What are you doing here? Mother's inside, and there are guards out."

"I have to talk to you."

"Come round to the servants' entrance. Quickly!"

I hurried around the building.

Dolcetta was waiting at the door, her arms folded over her chest. She wore a white nightshift. "You shouldn't be here."

"How could I stay away?"

"Mother says it's time for me to be married."

"I will gladly marry you."

"No, Beppo." She spoke my name tenderly. "I was foolish to lead you on."

"You didn't lead me on. I know you love me."

"I am to be married to an eligible suitor."

"Giovan Tomassoni?"

"Yes. In six months."

"To that snake? What about love?"

"I'm talking about *marriage*."

I pulled her against me and kissed her.

She kissed me back.

"Don't torment me, Beppo." Tears gathered and glistened at the corners of her eyes.

"Beppo!" Caravaggio hissed, somewhere in the darkness behind me.

I spun around.

He was perched on a garden wall, looking down at us.

"Sorry to interrupt your tryst, but we've run out of time. We must leave now!"

"*Now*, signore?" I could hardly contain my fury and despair.

"*Now!* You've put us both in jeopardy. Our boat is leaving for Malta at dawn. If we hurry, we can still make it aboard; I have the carriage waiting."

Footsteps crunched the gravel around the corner.

"I'll come back for you. Wait for me," I urged Dolcetta. I drew her into my embrace.

"I can't. I'm so sorry, Beppo." She pulled away and slipped back into the house.

"You there!" hollered a guard, lowering his pike.

I scrambled up over the wall, then turned for a last look. From an upper window, Fortunata glared down at me.

Our carriage flew down the Spaccanapoli toward Santa Lucia and the harbour. Dawn broke as we pulled up to the wharf alongside a ship whose sail bore a Maltese cross.

It was already unmoored, and the sailors were frantically waving us aboard. We raced up the gangplank and it was pulled up behind us. Several rowers in a small tugboat pulled our ship away from the dock.

Caravaggio, well pleased, gave me a hearty slap on the back. "Let's go below."

I breathed deeply, letting the salt air fill my nostrils. "You go. I'd rather stay up here."

"As you wish," he said. "Take your last look at Napoli."

He clambered below deck while I sat on the far side of the galley, watching the city recede into the distance.

Chapter Thirteen: Challenge

Cave tibi cane muto et aquâ silente.

Be on your guard against a silent dog and still water.

~Latin proverb

I had not been on a ship in years, and the constant rocking made me seasick. I spent the next several hours heaving up the contents of my stomach over the railing.

"You look green," Caravaggio observed.

"Doesn't all this tossing make you sick, signore?" I asked between spasms.

"Me? No. It's all in the legs, garzone."

"I wish I had your legs, signore," I replied glumly, retching once more into the sea below.

It was a full night and a day before the yellow promontories of Malta came into view. Sailing into the harbour of Valetta, we surveyed the fortifications and the cannons directed at would-be invaders. As we neared the dock, we cruised past an enormous, bright red warship. It sat low in the water, cannons pointing from its decks in all four directions. Most intimidating of all were the great white teeth painted onto the bow, like the jaws of a beast.

"The *Red Devil*: the most dreaded ship in the Mediterranean," Caravaggio informed me. "The Maltese knights use it to defend the seas against the Ottomans and to protect us from Turkish raiders and slavers."

We disembarked. I was grateful to be standing on the oily timbers of the dock. Two knights greeted us, their white tunics bearing the red, eight-pointed Maltese cross.

Caravaggio shook their hands heartily. "Fabrizio, you look like a beetle in all that armour. Fra Martelli, I see you have gained some weight!"

"Ha, ha! Michelangelo, you look like hell," Fra Martelli responded, embracing the painter. "Good to have you here. We'll have you strutting about in a tin suit of your own soon enough. The Grand Master has petitioned the Pope himself—and received approval!"

"He has?"

"Well, the Pope doesn't name you specifically. The approval is for 'a painter of renown' who will bring glory to our great Order."

"I am most relieved to hear it," Caravaggio boomed. "Beppo, let me introduce you to Fra Martelli and Fabrizio

Sforza Colonna, commander of the fleet. They are old friends of mine."

"Signor Merisi grew up with me in Caravaggio," General Colonna explained. "It's been a while, you scoundrel." He cuffed the painter playfully.

"Too bad you didn't come earlier," observed Fra Martelli. "I'm leaving for Syracuse in a week, to see to the harvest."

"Then I'll have to start your portrait right away. My servant, Beppo, will become my squire."

"Well, he's not a squire yet. He'll have to room with the pages, for now," countered the General.

Caravaggio and Fra Martelli went off together, and the General had someone escort me to my room in the Sant'Angelo fortress. I was placed with two younger boys. Our room was spacious but sparsely furnished. It held four beds, one of which was piled with sheets and blankets. A single arched window let in light from the west.

"Where do you come from?" one of the young pages asked me.

"Roma," I said. "Before that, Sardinia. I'm Beppo."

"If anyone else asks, better just to say 'Roma.' I'm Christoforo," he added, extending his hand.

"Alphonse," said the other. "We're brothers. Our father is Cesare d'Este, Duke of Modena. Who's your father?"

"I—well, I'm here accompanying Signor Merisi da Caravaggio. He's to be knighted, and I'm going to be his squire."

"The painter? So it's true!" Christoforo exclaimed. "Our

families paid a lot of money for us to be groomed as squires, while you are getting in on his merit. Some of the boys might resent that."

"Some of the knights too," remarked Alphonse.

The next morning, I was issued baggy black pantaloons, red stockings and a fitted black shirt with a small ruff at the collar. I thought that the page's outfit looked more like a choirboy's attire, but I dressed without argument. Then Christoforo and Alphonse led me along a raised walkway overlooking a courtyard. Below, the squires were receiving long-sword fighting lessons from a knight.

Pah! They are just beginners!

We joined a group of pages for lessons in manners: how to bow—lower for a lady than for a knight; how to hold deliveries aloft—elbows and back straight, palms up; how to walk noiselessly within chambers—balls of the feet first; and how and when to speak when addressed—"Yes, my good lord; no, Monsignor; as your good pleasure dictates, Grand Master." We practised over and over, hour upon hour. No swords, no guns, not one word about how to take off a Turk's head.

The lessons for pages and squires alike ended at midday. I was told that a meal would be served to us in the common hall. I hadn't eaten since the night before, and my hunger pangs were as insistent as an impatient dog clawing at the door.

As Christoforo, Alphonse and I approached the dining hall, a group of squires gathered in front of us.

"Keep your eyes down," advised Christoforo. "Don't say anything."

I raised my chin defiantly.

"What have we here, masters?" cried one of the squires, deliberately blocking our way. "Going somewhere, *garzoni*?"

My companions kept their heads down and their eyes glued to the floor.

"We are headed to the hall for the midday meal," I replied calmly, looking him in the eye.

"Do you hear that, Giorgio?" he laughed. "He wants a meal!" He strolled closer to me and growled. "Well, garzone, it so happens that the knights and the Grand Master, they eat first. After that come the squires—that's us. Then we feed the dogs, the cats, the rats and any Turks still languishing in the dungeons. And then," he trumpeted, "we piss on what's left and give it to you."

The squires laughed uproariously.

"Don't answer him," Christoforo whispered to me beneath the din. "Lorenzo's looking for an excuse to fight you."

I ignored his warning. "That sounds most agreeable, signorina," I addressed the squire. "But when you squat over the scraps, don't forget to lift your skirt."

The squires raised their eyebrows and clicked their tongues in amazement.

"Oh, you are a brash one, aren't you? I see you need some lessons in how to be a page." Lorenzo grabbed a sword from Giorgio and swiftly passed it to me. It was a long-sword; I needed both hands to wield it.

"Don't!" counselled Christoforo. "Lorenzo will say

you attacked him, and he'll get away with it. They always do."

Hmm. Sounds like good advice. I pointed the sword down.

"No, no, garzone," Lorenzo taunted me. "You must hold it *up*, thus!" He forced my sword up. "Can't have the point falling limp!"

I dropped my left foot back and shifted my weight.

"Come on, then! Give us a downstroke."

He is goading me. Watch and wait. I remained perfectly still.

"Come on, garzone, we haven't got all day."

Still I made no move.

Lorenzo swung at me. But he was off-balance. I stepped out of his path and stuck out my foot as he sailed past, tripping him. He sprawled onto the ground.

"That's a very good lesson," I said. "Perhaps we can do this again another day—garzone."

Lorenzo rose and lunged at me. I side-stepped him neatly, grabbed the pommel of his sword, and rammed it into his chest. It knocked him down.

"What's going on here?" Caravaggio's voice thundered behind me. Fra Martelli was standing next to him.

"This—this page," sputtered Lorenzo, "attacked me without provocation. Isn't that right, Giorgio?"

"With two swords?" queried Fra Martelli.

"Y—yes, my lord," Lorenzo quavered. "He stole them from us."

Caravaggio turned to me. "Is this true?"

"It is true that I disarmed him. But he told me that I needed a lesson and left me no choice. I merely obliged him—and defended myself." With a low bow, I returned the swords to the squires.

"You let this page make a fool of you, Lorenzo?" Fra Martelli enquired.

Lorenzo glowered at me. "He took advantage of me, signore."

"Ha! Two weeks' cleaning duty. Now, off to your meal." Fra Martelli and Caravaggio headed into the dining hall.

"I'll fix you," Lorenzo snarled, signalling Giorgio to follow him.

Chapter Fourteen: Under Attack

Nec parcit imbellis juventae
Poplitibus timidoque tergo.

The youth in vain would fly from fate's attack
With trembling knees and terror at his back.

~Quintus Horatius Flaccus (Horace),
trans. By Jonathan Swift

Later that day, I was called to appear before the Grand Master, Alof de Wignacourt. Lorenzo and Giorgio emerged from the room as I entered the hall. They jostled me as they passed. I knocked at the door, and a bearded knight ushered me in.

The Grand Master was sitting on a throne, under a white flag with the red Maltese cross. His red beard and close-cropped hair were tinged with white. The knight assumed his place between Caravaggio and General Colonna, who sat next to the Grand Master.

The Grand Master gestured for me to approach. A scowl sat on his hard broad face. "We hear you've been involved in some trouble. What do you have to say for yourself?"

Suddenly, all the instruction I'd been receiving in formal modes of address became useful. "My humble apology, most illustrious Highness and Grand Master thrice illuminated. Perhaps this kind of trouble could be avoided if you were to make me a squire. Then I would be on an even footing with the others and thus would command their respect."

"Even footing?" My interrogator looked incredulous. "Lorenzo's father is the Marchese di Palermo. Who is *your* father?"

"My father . . ." *My father was an Andalusian who died of the plague. And my stepfather was a Sardinian merchant who sold me for a debt.*

Caravaggio broke in. "He's orphaned, Grand Master."

General Colonna leaned over to the Grand Master and whispered in his ear.

The Grand Master considered for a moment, then nodded. "General Colonna has suggested that you accompany his vicar to Venezia. You will serve as his page and escort. If you discharge your duties properly, you will be promoted to squire upon your return."

I glanced at Caravaggio, seeking his approval. He nodded.

"Signore, I—"

"Tch, tch." The Grand Master held up a heavy finger. "Go now. Gather your things. And see if you can avoid another fight before your departure."

The Vicar of the Venezia Priory of St. John Hospitaller was an old man, thin and frail, with a long face and a neck like a stork's. He ordered me to carry his trunks onto the ship.

Our second day at sea was rough and windy. Large swells heaved the caravel perilously upward before the bow crashed down into the trough of the waves, sending up a wall of spray on both sides of the vessel. Yet the Vicar stood amidships the whole time, his hands clasped behind his back.

I had to grip the railing to keep from sliding overboard. The sailors scrambled around me, shouting to one another over the roar of the wind and the breaking seas.

Gradually, my stomach became accustomed to the boat's motion. On the third day, the winds died and the seas were calm. Our sails were up. I awoke to the clamour of footsteps on deck and shouts of "Corsair! Corsair! Pirates!"

Two galley ships—their oars dipping in unison, their lateen sails wrapped around their booms—were gaining upon us rapidly.

"Barbary ships," announced the Vicar, as I hurried over to him. "We'll not escape a fight today." He must have seen the look of terror on my face, for he gripped my forearm and said, "Always be prepared to die; then you'll know you're truly alive."

As the corsairs closed in on us, men hurried to their battle stations, and our port-side cannons opened fire. But the galley simply shifted starboard, so that our broadsides missed their targets. The pirates' first shot exploded through our upper deck, rocking the ship. The attackers threw nets over our gunnels and boarded the caravel, their curved swords flashing in the sun.

The Vicar hurried me inside his cabin and pulled out a long chest from under his bed. He opened it to reveal a sword and several wheel-lock *pistole*, magnificent guns that fired with flints and required no wicks. He must have noticed my amazement. "One of the benefits of serving under the Knights: superb weapons!" He stuffed the barrel of a *pistola* with gunpowder and wadding, then packed in a bullet. Seizing a sword too, he burst out the door into the fray.

I grabbed a sword and ran after him.

Our men were engaged in furious battle. A sailor hit the deck hard, clutching a ghastly gash on his neck. Another man's arm was nearly severed. Blood spurted everywhere.

The Vicar hacked his way into the fight and put a bullet into a pirate's head. He slashed the legs of two more attackers, who fell at his feet.

There was a terrible mêlée of gunfire, clashing swords and shrieks. Our sailors were outnumbered. I ran back to the Vicar's quarters, threw down my sword, and grasped two *pistole*. Once I had packed them with gunpowder, I pried open a case of lead bullets and loaded the guns. It was a sloppy job, and gunpowder dusted the floor all around me. I ripped off a corner of my shirt, tore the fabric into two pieces and moistened them in my mouth. Then I grabbed a ramrod and packed the cloth strips down the barrels.

All at once, the shouting on deck was replaced by heavy footsteps and the sound of hatches being flung open. Someone unlatched the door of the Vicar's cabin. As it swung open, I cocked back the hammer of the *pistola* and fired.

A pirate fell into the cabin, dead. But another rushed in

behind him and knocked the gun out of my hands. "Well, well, *cos'è questo?*" What's this?

An Italian!

He grabbed me by the collar and forced me up onto the deck.

Chapter Fifteen: The Pasha

Il più delle volte le avversità non vadino sole.

In the majority of cases, misfortunes do not come alone.

~Francesco Guicciardini

Carnage. The deck was red and slick with blood.

While the corsair's cargo was transferred to our caravel, the dead were cast overboard. I winced at the sound of each splash. The older captives, including the Vicar, were chained together, alongside the starboard gunwale.

"*Kheir Pasha*," called the Italian, clutching me by the collar. "Here is another!" A fearsome figure turned to face me and bound my wrists. He wore a turban, a cape, and a long tunic that billowed over loose pants. His black moustache and beard stood out against swarthy skin.

Suddenly, he flicked a golden sword, and one of the pirates abruptly shoved the Vicar into the sea, as if he were a sack of flour. The chain dragged the others over the gunwale, each screaming, "Mercy, mercy! Please—no!" as he slid over the edge and into the watery depths.

I was hauled below the galley's main deck. There I saw the rowers, chained to their benches. The acrid smells of urine and sweat brought my stomach up to my throat.

Now that the battle was over, the pirates sat idly. They were bearded and shirtless, their backs glistening with an oily film of sweat.

Two chairs faced them: one held a drum; the other, a whip.

The pirates shackled me next to a vacant-eyed youth.

A string of men had been put to work bringing chests and barrels up from the hold to the top deck. We watched them in silence. I could not tell how long we remained there in the semi-darkness. After a while, two people descended. One was a boy, shirtless, shoeless, brown-skinned and thin. The other—cloaked, booted and wearing a black hat—was the Italian who fawned upon the Pasha. He forced the boy into a seated position and chained him to the others. The boy immediately began picking at the rusty head of a spike in the floorboard.

The Italian released my manacles. He laughed menacingly. "I'm taking you to see the Pasha," he announced.

I climbed the steep ladder with difficulty. My captor steered me by the arm to a small cabin at the rear of the galley. He knocked at the door, opened it and pushed me through.

The Pasha pointed to my wrists, which the Italian promptly freed. Then the Pasha gestured to him to leave. He nodded and turned away, closing the door behind him.

The cabin contained a bed and two rows of cushioned benches that tapered toward the vessel's narrow stern. A heavy table bolted to the floor was piled high on one side with various maps, charts and a sextant. In the corner was an ornate wooden chest, upon which rested the Vicar's pistol box.

The Pasha sat down, scrutinizing me. He made a twirling motion with his index finger, apparently commanding me to turn around. I stood still.

"Turn," he commanded, in a thick Berber accent.

"You—you speak Italian?" I stammered.

"Only when I need to. Now turn."

"What do you want with me?"

The Pasha rose and stepped toward me. He regarded me sternly, then pulled out a thin rod from his belt and cracked it hard across my elbow. The pain brought me to my knees.

"Maybe I want nothing. Maybe I want that you row. Maybe I sell you. Now, turn!"

This time, I complied. I stood and turned in a full circle.

He sat back down. "Again," he commanded.

I turned again.

"You fifteen?"

I realized then that somehow I had missed my birthday. "I'm sixteen."

"I like you, boy." He wagged his finger at me, looking down its length as though he were sighting down the barrel of a gun. "Maybe you get good price, yes?"

"At a slave market? You're a fiend!"

"You are fierce, angry, I see—strong to fight. Maybe not good for market. Maybe only for row oars. Or maybe I break you first, like horse, make you eat from my hand."

I swallowed hard, my body tense. *Could I get to the chest and the loaded pistole?*

"Face wall." The Pasha stood up again.

This is my only chance. I bolted and flung open the armoury chest.

Empty!

Click.

I turned and stared at the Pasha in horror. He had pulled a pistola from his sash, cocked the wheel-lock and was pointing it at my chest.

"You look for this?" He pushed my face against the wall and held the gun to my head. "Stay like this, or I tie you like goat."

He put the arm of the pistola back into the safety position and traced the muscles in my back with the gun handle.

There was a knock at the door.

The Pasha grunted. The Italian entered with the brown-skinned boy. His wrists were still bound, and his hands were tightly clasped.

"He insisted on seeing you, honourable Pasha."

The Pasha nodded approvingly, seeming both pleased and surprised.

The boy knelt down before him and spoke softly. The Pasha patted the boy's head in an almost fatherly way, then signalled to the Italian to withdraw.

"Now I show you," the Pasha gloated. "This boy here fight before, but now he learn. Do not fight with Kheir Pasha. Do what Kheir Pasha say." He lifted the boy's chin triumphantly. "This boy know now that Kheir Pasha is master."

The boy suddenly thrust his clasped hands upward at the Pasha's belly, then over and over again at his chest with savage force. The Pasha's smile twisted in agony. Blood poured from his gaping wounds. His body shuddered. After a long minute, he fell forward, dead.

The boy dropped a bloody spike nearly half-a-foot long onto the floor and held up his bound hands toward me. I searched feverishly for a knife among the Pasha's things, and used it to sever the ropes around the boy's wrists. He touched his forehead with his fingertips, which I interpreted as a sign of gratitude.

"We need to free the others," I told him. I pointed at the door.

He pointed at himself. "Malak," he said, tapping his chest. "Malak."

I nodded. "Beppo," I said, tapping mine. I held up my wrists, first together, then apart, miming the suggested act. Again, I pointed at the door. He squinted, trying to understand. I picked up the pistola, motioned to the sword on the table and pointed below the deck. Finally, he nodded.

I opened the door a crack and peered out. The sea was still. The second corsair galley had released its ropes and had sailed off, but my ship remained fastened to the Pasha's. A small group of pirates, exhausted from the fighting, was lounging on the upper deck.

I closed the cabin door and tucked the pistola into my waist, at the small of my back. Then I stripped the Pasha of his clothes.

"You Pasha, me prisoner," I instructed the boy, gesturing.

I handed the Pasha's pantaloons and cape to Malak.

The tyrant's shirt was far too bloody to be used, so I gave Malak my own shirt instead. I watched the door as he wrapped the Pasha's turban around his head, then stood aghast as he tore out a fistful of the Pasha's beard. He daubed the hairs in the pooled blood on the floor, and pressed them to his chin until they stuck. Lastly, he grabbed the Pasha's sword.

I turned to open the door, but Malak grasped my arm and pointed to my hands. I realized that we would have to bind them if I were to play my role convincingly. He wrapped a rope loosely around my wrists, opened the door, and gripped me by the arm as if I were his captive. He marched me in front of him onto the deck, illuminated now only by a sliver of moon.

I kept my head down as we proceeded to the hatch. One pirate who observed our progress called over another and pointed at us. Malak gripped my left arm more tightly. I slipped my right hand out of the ropes and reached around to the pistola at my back. We descended hastily through the hatch.

I hadn't considered the darkness below. The rowers' deck was pitch black. I had thought of the night as a cloak, not as a blindfold. After our eyes had adjusted to the dark, we advanced toward the silhouettes of young and old men slumped in sleep on the benches.

My companion roused them quietly. But we had no key with which to set them free. We could only wait.

It was some time before I heard the first heavy footstep on the ladder's top rung. The pirate held a lantern aloft. Shadows danced madly around the cabin as the lantern swung during his descent. Keys jangled at his hip. As soon as he reached the floor, I pulled out my gun and pointed it at his chest.

Malak leaped forward, pressed his sword to the pirate's throat, and covered his mouth before he could cry out. I bound our prisoner's hands and then gagged him, as Malak's sword hovered. We relieved the pirate of his keys and sat him down among the rowers.

We worked feverishly to release everyone's manacles.

"Is this it?" barked one of the young rowers who had been captured with me. "Is this your plan? Boys and slaves against armed pirates?"

"Keep your voice down," I hissed. "This isn't a plan; it just happened. But we do have a chance, if we can make our way over to the caravel. There aren't many pirates aboard her. We can overpower them, cut the ropes and sail away. Without the help of rowers, they won't be able to catch us."

"Brilliant," another galley slave remarked bitterly, "except for one thing."

"What's that?"

"How can we *get* to the other boat without getting cut to pieces? We have no weapons. And that," he said, pointing to the hatch, "is the only way out. Congratulations. You haven't freed us; you've killed us!"

"We can get to the armoury before they know what's happening. Here, get dressed."

I strode over to the captive pirate and stripped him. With Malak's sword at his throat, he offered no resistance.

The scoffer donned each of the pirate's garments as I tossed them to him.

"The swords are stored in a locker near the forecastle," another rower offered. "Where the crew sleeps. I saw them as we were being bound."

I turned back to the scoffer. "If the pirates are asleep, we can arm ourselves and then chain the forecastle shut. They'll be locked in before they realize what's happening. Then we only have to fight the ones who are up on deck. And we can take them by surprise."

Resolutely, I ascended the ladder. Several of the freed men followed me, sneaking past the rogues who lay sprawled asleep on deck. We stole into the Pasha's cabin, where we helped ourselves to splendid weapons. Then we crept toward the locker.

Chapter Sixteen: The Red Devil

O misera compagna sventurata,
Qual peccato fu quel che t' ha condotta
A correr sì com' acqua a fiotta a fiotta?

Oh, wretched, luckless companion,
What sin was yours as to condemn you
To flow like water in wave after wave?

~Giovanni Boccaccio

As more of my compatriots surged up the ladder from their cramped slave deck, I directed them to the cache of swords in the locker. Clutching one of the Vicar's rapiers, I whispered, "Chain the forecastle."

Two of the rowers tried to secure the door, but the chain clanked loudly. Alerted, the pirates who had been resting within smashed open the hatch from the other side and rushed out, brandishing bottles and daggers. It wasn't long before they had seized swords from the armoury chest.

"The caravel," I gasped, grabbing Malak and pointing to the Vicar's ship.

He nodded.

"Stop fighting and make for the other ship!" I shouted to the freed rowers.

The swaying hulls of the two vessels were secured to each other with thick, tarred ropes. I jumped onto the plank leading to the caravel and scrambled up it on all fours.

A curved scimitar flashed above me. I hurled myself from the plank to the deck and whipped the pistola from my waistband. I shot wildly in the direction of the scimitar-wielding knave—and was astonished when an entirely different figure tumbled down from above.

Malak and another boy bounded off the gangplank behind me. Two pirates charged us, their blades slicing the air around my head.

I parried and thrust with my rapier, but it was knocked from my hand.

Two more of the former galley slaves jumped from the gangplank, and forced one of the pirates overboard. Malak shouted something. I ducked. At the same instant, a gunshot cracked from behind me. The other pirate fell. I looked up and glimpsed the Italian, lowering his matchlock arquebus.

Who did he intend to shoot?

We had won possession of the caravel.

"Untie the ships," the Italian bellowed, pointing at the galley.

Together we untied the heavy hemp rope joining the two vessels and pitched the gangplank into the sea.

The Italian kicked out the wedge securing the loaded cannon, tipping its nose downward toward the corsair. He removed the smouldering wick from his matchlock, held it to the touch hole, and turned his head away. The blast washed over me like a wave, sending us reeling. A cannonball punched through the corsair's upper deck and exploded, ripping the vessel in two.

I shook my head to clear the ringing in my ears.

"They're finished," he said, with a grim smile.

We watched silently as the wreck slipped beneath the sea, a bubbling froth marking its location. I scanned the waves, but saw no survivors.

"Now *I* have control over this vessel and its contents," asserted the Italian, jamming more wadding down the barrel of his arquebus. "The pirate's code, boy! Normally, the shares are split among the survivors, but as I seem to be the only surviving crew member, there will be only *one* share. Mine."

I stooped to retrieve my rapier. "We beg to differ," I declared grandly, gesturing toward Malak and the dark-skinned boys crowding behind him. I was pleased to see that they still had their weapons.

The Italian laughed nastily. "I don't think so. I think your friends will remain loyal to me right up to the moment that I sell them at the market." He shouted something in Berber to the youths, and pointed at the mast. They immediately pulled the ropes to unfurl the sails, which began billowing in the wind. Then he raised his gun and pointed it at me. "Put down your sword."

"Aren't you forgetting something?" I asked him.

He followed the line of my gaze toward the empty serpentine on his gun, and then toward the extinguished wick next to the cannon. "No matter," he growled, tossing his gun aside and grabbing the dead pirate's sword.

I lunged at him, but he parried my thrust—then slashed my left shoulder. Blood ran down my arm and dripped off my hand. As he sliced the air with his blade again, I pitched away, rolled and jumped to my feet. I dodged and parried. At his next thrust, I succeeded in grabbing his sword. I flung it away and, with all my might, plunged my rapier into his chest.

The Italian let loose a stream of curses and tried to twist free of the blade. His struggles only worsened his situation. Agonized minutes later, he died.

I pulled my rapier from his chest, avoiding his frozen stare.

Malak gazed at my bloody shoulder and shook his head.

"I'll be fine," I assured him, with a confidence I did not feel. I knew I needed a doctor.

I trudged over to the caravel's gunwale.

Soon, the first streaks of daylight appeared on the horizon. The sea was as calm as a glass plate. Malak and the others searched the ship for food and water. To our dismay, there was not much to be found. Although our caravel was loaded with all of the corsair's treasures, most of the food provisions had sunk with the galley.

We ate sparingly. I doubted that we would survive long enough to enjoy our riches.

On the second day, I contracted a fever. I drifted in and out of sleep. Malak tried to cleanse my oozing wound with salt water.

On the third day, he shook me awake. *"Yella! Yella!"* he screeched, helping me onto my feet. I staggered out the cabin door, my shoulder stiff and radiating pain. Malak pointed out over the sea. On the horizon, a large vessel sailed low on the water. It was painted bright red, and bristled with oars.

The Red Devil.

Malak's eyes were wide with fear. *"Besora'a! Besora'a!"* He and the others started running frantically to and fro, gathering up whatever supplies they could. They worked desperately at the ropes to lower the caravel's dinghy into the water.

I raised my hand, to signal that they should not be so alarmed, that the *Red Devil* belonged to friends of mine. But I was overcome with dizziness. I passed out on the deck and floated into a black abyss.

I am weightless. I am swimming underwater. Light ripples over my skin, and everything is blue. The underside of a small boat breaks the surface above me. I reach toward it, then pull myself up and into the boat. Dolcetta is there. We are in a gondola laden with pillows. She wraps me in her arms and I am soon dry in the warm sun. She lays her head on my chest. I try to speak, but she lifts her head, smiles, and touches her finger to my lips. Then she kisses my cheek.

Cold water splashed onto my face.

"Welcome back, garzone," said General Colonna.

I was propped upright with pillows. A man in a dark robe sat on a stool next to me and peeled a bandage off my shoulder. The General stood at the foot of the bed.

The air smelled of brine. A seabird squawked.

"Where am I?" I asked the man in the dark robe. "Who are you?"

"You're aboard the *Red Devil*. I'm Doctor Falzone. You have an infection, but your fever is under control."

A dark, crusted line ran along my shoulder, like a ribbon of dried kelp.

"Where are the others?"

"The others?" queried the General. "You mean the Italian pirate? Dead, I'm pleased to report. Apparently by your hand. Rodolfo Calabrese was a notorious traitor. You're a credit, my boy."

"Thank you, General. And what happened to the other boys?"

"There was no one else aboard the caravel. We have it under tow."

Malak and his companions must have decided that it was better to risk the sea in a dinghy than to endure the Maltese slave market.

Haltingly, I recounted my adventures to the General.

"If what you say is true—"

"It *is* true!"

"In that case, this rightfully belongs to you." The General placed a small leather-bound ledger on the bed next to me. "We took an inventory of everything that the Barbary pirates loaded onto the caravel."

I opened the book and scanned a lengthy list of weapons, gold, jewels, silks and spices.

"I don't understand."

"Since you are the sole survivor of the caravel, the contents are yours, by every law of the sea. You are now a very rich young man. No doubt, a celebration is in order when we return to Malta. But more of that tomorrow."

I was flabbergasted, but all I could think of to say was, "When will I see Signor Caravaggio?"

The General glanced at the doctor, who continued to dab at my shoulder.

"All things in good time," replied the General. "Our painter is not going anywhere just now. As for you, it is important that you rest."

Once we had docked, two men carried me off the ship in a litter. I was placed in a carriage and driven to General Colonna's villa, where a sumptuous meal and a comfortable bed awaited.

The next morning, I felt revived. My fever was gone and, although my wound was painful to the touch, my discomfort was tolerable.

Someone knocked at the bedroom door.

"Come in."

A young page entered. "The General requests that you meet him down at the pier to review the caravel's inventory. A carriage will take you over there after breakfast. Please follow me."

I slipped on a loose shirt, and followed the page to the veranda. When I had finished eating, the carriage brought me to the harbour. The General was there, in the company of several Maltese knights.

"Buongiorno," General Colonna said warmly. "Beppo, allow me to introduce you to Fra Marc'Aurelio and Fra Francesco Buonarotti, whom I have invited to join us today."

I bowed.

"Are you feeling better?"

"Sì, signore. Grazie."

"Good. Then let us go aboard."

We climbed the gangway to the caravel's deck, where several chests full of gold and silver were displayed.

"This is quite a cache, Beppo," observed the General.

A wine barrel hoisted from the hold was deposited gently onto the deck.

"You are a fortunate young man," Fra Marc'Aurelio remarked.

"God has smiled on you," added Signor Buonarotti.

The next wine barrel to be brought up from the hold shifted and smashed onto the deck. Books went flying everywhere.

"There's no wine in these barrels!" the General sputtered in dismay. Seizing an axe, he splintered the first barrel. He reached into it and withdrew a book. "*Don Quijote de la Mancha,*" he read, utterly perplexed. He leafed through its pages and tossed the volume to me. "I have never seen books in barrels before!"

I almost laughed. "*I* have, signore. They're fakes, of course. If it weren't for books like these, Signor Caravaggio and I would still be in Roma. Where *is* he? Why hasn't he come to see me?"

The three men exchanged glances.

"I'm afraid that would—ah, prove difficult," General Colonna stammered.

Chapter Seventeen:
The Death Cell

Il sole indarno il chiaro dì vi mena;
Che non vi può mai penetrar coi raggi,
Sì gli è la via da folti rami tronca:
E quivi entra sottera una spelonca.

Thither the circling sun without avail
Conveys the cheerful daylight: for no breach
The rays can make through boughs spread thickly round;
And it is here a cave runs under ground.

~Ludovico Ariosto

General Colonna pointed up toward limestone blocks rising from the rocky point. "Deep in the heart of the Fortress is a bell-shaped pit, eleven feet deep, capped by an iron lid. It's a cell known as the *Guva*. That's where Caravaggio is."

"What has he done now?"

"There was a brawl, and a knight was shot," Fra Marc'Aurelio said, shaking his head. "Lorenzo, one of the squires, started the altercation. But for Caravaggio to shoot a knight . . ."

"Can't any of you help him?"

The three men looked at each other and shrugged.

"Beppo, I would be pleased to take you on as my squire," faltered the General. "You've got spirit. Four years at my side, and you'll be a worthy knight before you're twenty-one years old."

"Forgive me, General, but you speak as if Caravaggio is already dead."

"I'm sorry. His imprisonment has been ordered by the Grand Master himself. Caravaggio's prospects are grim."

A gust of wind sprang up, tossing the heavy ship as it sat anchored in the harbour. The General ambled over to a chest of gold coins and scooped handfuls of them into a small leather sack. "Here," he said, handing me the sack. "Perhaps you can find some consolation in this."

"Perhaps. Thank you." I felt dejected.

"As for the remainder, I'll have it sent to my villa, where it will be under lock and key until you determine what you want to do with it."

"With your leave, General, I'd like to return to the mainland. Just a short sojourn—to fulfill a promise."

"Of course."

When I returned to my room at General Colonna's villa, it was late afternoon. I found a letter waiting on my bed, and tore open the envelope at once. It was from Dolcetta, written in the hand of a professional scribe.

Dear Beppo,

I have no way of knowing if this letter will reach you. Surely you know that you are the love of my life. I will hold you in my heart forever. Yet my mother has arranged for my marriage to Giovan Tomassoni at the church of San Luigi dei Francesi on April 10. I will be staying at the residence of the Duke of Parma before the wedding. Save me from this terrible fate, my brave hidalgo.

Yours even now,
Dolcetta Fiammini

I would have to change my plans. I put some of my newly acquired riches into a small purse and headed to the docks, to book passage for Roma.

Merchant ships crowded along the pier. The wharves were thronged with sailors, soldiers and labourers. Two knights sauntered by. One of them studied my face before turning away.

I met with the captain of a small *barchetta*. A burly man with thick arms and shoulders, Captain Matteo seemed even-tempered and friendly.

I dropped my purse of gold coins onto a wooden crate. "I need to be in Roma before April tenth."

"Of course, signore. We sail in four days."

"And no questions!"

"Of course."

"There will be two of us. I will send our things ahead." I emptied half of the purse's contents onto the table. "This is yours; you will receive the other half of your payment when we arrive in Roma. Meet us with a skiff at the dock below the fortress on Friday morning, when the bell tolls one."

The captain shovelled the coins into his palm and smiled broadly. "Sì."

Once the sun had set, the Fortress looked more forbidding than ever. Its stone walls ran straight up from the steep cliff face. *Poor Caravaggio.*

I spent the next three days making preparations for the voyage, including the posting of two letters. One was to Cardinal del Monte in Roma, explaining again that it was Ranuccio Tomassoni who had killed Constantino. The other message, requesting refuge for Caravaggio, was addressed to the knight Fra Martelli, who had left Malta for Syracuse.

I packed a trunk with clothing and two of Caravaggio's canvasses and delivered it to the dock. The sun had just dipped below the horizon when General Colonna summoned me. I knocked at the door of his rooms, and he welcomed me in.

"Everything is arranged, Beppo?"

"Sì, signore. I leave tomorrow."

"And you have all that you need?"

"Only one more thing to load, signore."

"And what about Caravaggio?"

"I'm sure that God will provide for him."

"Take this with you." The General handed me a small envelope, sealed with red wax and bearing the impression of his signet ring. "It is a letter of introduction, in the event that anyone in Napoli detains you. You also will find an accounting of the gold and jewels you have left in my care. You can draw against this through the Knights' Priory in Napoli—or anywhere else, should you need to."

"Grazie, signore."

The night was almost unnaturally still. A ship's bell tolled in the distance. The sound seemed to skip like a stone over the water. The moon cast odd shadows along the walkways leading to the Guva. At the end of the corridor, a massive door, reinforced with steel, barred my way.

I carried my sword, a length of rope, and a bag containing food and a bottle of wine. Concealing the rope inside my coat, I approached the Guva's door and knocked. The circular cover of the Judas hole slid back, revealing an eye.

"What do you want?"

"I've brought food for the prisoner."

"Who are you?"

"A page, signore."

"Go away. He already ate." The peephole cover closed.

I banged on the door again. "This food is from the Grand Master himself."

The cover opened again. "The Grand Master?"

I held up the bottle of wine, and the guard unbolted the door. "Give it here," he said, stepping out into the corridor.

I grabbed his outstretched hand, jerked it sharply, and hit him squarely in the forehead with the bottle. It shattered, and he crumpled to the stone floor with a thud.

"Signor Caravaggio?" I called softly. "Can you hear me?"

There was low moan from deep inside the hole. "Beppo, is that you?"

"Yes. Let's get you out of here!"

I dragged the unconscious guard behind the door, removed the key ring from his belt, and shut the door behind me. Then I unlocked and lifted the Guva's lid. After tying one end of the rope to a column, I yanked a torch from the wall and held it over the opening. Below, Caravaggio lay crumpled in a heap. I wedged the torch into a crack in the wall above the hole and lowered the rope.

"Climb up!"

The rope twisted and swung. Grunts echoed from the hole, but Caravaggio did not emerge. Several minutes elapsed.

"Hurry!" I urged.

All at once, I heard shouting and running footsteps. There was a jangling of keys. The door was flung open, and two knights in tunics and mail hurtled in.

"You there! You're under arrest!" one of them bellowed.

I drew my sword from its sheath and faced them both. They unsheathed their weapons in response.

"Put that down, boy, or this will be the last breath you take," one of them warned. He levelled his sword at my head.

I peered into the pit's opening. Caravaggio must have retreated into its shadows.

"Two knights? That seems a fair fight," I remarked dryly.

The taller knight snorted. "Prepare to meet your Maker!"

I backed up against a column—and was astonished when Caravaggio stepped from behind it. Evidently he had scaled the rope during my anxious few minutes' vigil, and had slipped into a concealed spot an instant before the knights burst in. He leaped onto one of them, toppling him easily. I slashed in the other knight's direction. He shrank back. Caravaggio stooped to pick up the sword of the fallen knight and pointed it at his throat.

"Yield!"

"You will never escape, you villain!" the defeated knight spat out.

"Suppose you say you were never here, and that fool of a jailer was entirely to blame for my escape," Caravaggio advised. "Or would you rather die at my feet, here and now? The choice is yours."

"Ronaldo, sheathe your weapon," muttered the knight on the floor.

Ronaldo grudgingly lowered his sword and stepped away from me.

"Give us ten minutes," Caravaggio decreed. "Then you can sound the alarm."

"Andiamo," I urged. "Let's get out of here."

Chapter Eighteen: A Fool's Errand

Sempre che l' inimico è più possente,
Più, chi perde, accettabile ha la scusa.

The stronger the enemy, the better the excuse of the one
who has been defeated.

~Ludovico Ariosto

Caravaggio led me across the courtyard.

"Where are we going?" I whispered urgently. "We need to hurry to the dock!"

Caravaggio put a finger to his lips and ushered me into the grand hall. There, a flicker of torchlight illuminated the largest canvas I had ever seen. A nearby table was covered with pots and brushes.

"*The Beheading of Saint John the Baptist*," my master proclaimed.

The painting depicted an executioner poised over

the gravely wounded prophet, about to decapitate him. A shocked witness raised her hands to her face, while another woman held a golden tray on which to receive the severed head.

The violence and pathos of the scene took my breath away. But my anxiety returned a moment later. "Signore, we must be at the dock when the bell tolls one."

Caravaggio dipped his finger into a pot of red paint and signed the canvas as if in the blood gushing from John the Baptist's neck.

"Perfect," he pronounced.

"We must go—now!" I seized him by the arm and propelled him down a long series of stone switchbacks. Then we hurried along a rocky promontory toward the ramp that led to the loading dock at the water's edge.

Captain Matteo waved to us from a skiff.

An hour later, we were safely aboard his small barchetta, *The Tiger*, flying the Maltese flag.

"A few moments more and the sails will be up," the captain assured us.

Soon we were sailing into the open sea.

Caravaggio slept for hours. When he awoke, I told him about Dolcetta's letter and the riches that I had acquired from my encounter with the pirates.

"Looks like you've learned something from me, after all! But you're sticking your neck out by going back to Roma.

For what: a girl? As usual, you haven't thought this through. I cannot help you."

"I don't need your help. I fought off the pirates *without* you."

"This is a different kind of battle. Tomassoni has many very powerful connections."

"Too bad. My mind's made up. Fra Martelli will take you in. He has a villa in Syracuse; you'll be safe there. It's all been arranged."

"In exchange for another tasteless commission?"

"As always."

We were a day and a night at sea before putting into port at Syracuse, on the nearby island of Sicily. It was unusually cool for April, and the sky threatened rain. The crewmen unloaded the painter's trunk and deposited it on the dock next to Fra Martelli, who had come with three servants and a carriage to greet us.

"Welcome to Syracuse, Signor Caravaggio," announced our new host, as we descended the gangway.

The painter took his friend's hand and shook it again and again. "I wish it were under different circumstances."

"I am glad to offer you my home as a place of refuge. You must have had an exhausting ordeal."

"Sì. Grazie."

The servants hoisted my master's trunk onto the carriage and Fra Martelli gestured for Caravaggio to join him inside.

My master turned and clapped me on the shoulder. "This is a fool's errand, Beppo. You should reconsider."

"If it is a fool's errand, I'm the right one for the job, master."

I held out my hand, and he grasped it. Then he pulled me in close and whispered into my ear. "You were never my servant, *capisce?*" Understand? He stepped back and winked. "You are my friend."

He climbed into Fra Martelli's carriage, and I made my way back up the gangplank.

I watched the crewmen unfasten the ropes from the moorings. *I hope this is the end of Caravaggio's troubles—and of mine, as well.*

A sudden downpour forced me below deck.

Two days later, we dropped anchor at the port of Civitavecchia just before noon. Large ships sat anchored outside the harbour, so numerous that they looked like an invading armada. Within the hour, a two-man skiff pulled alongside our ship. A muscular rower asked about our cargo and consulted a ledger. Captain Matteo asked him when we would dock.

"*Domani,*" the port officer answered. Tomorrow.

"But I have to be in Roma in three days!" I protested. I produced a small purse and tossed it to the rower.

"In that case, you can dock immediately."

We pulled up to the wharf. A group of dockworkers boarded the ship and carried the goods onto a barge hitched to a team of oxen on shore. The captain and I climbed down off the ship and onto the barge, which began the slow drag up the river to Roma.

It took almost as long to be pulled up the Tiber as it did to sail from Syracuse to Civitavecchia. But at last we approached the large central arch of the Ponte Cestio.

I stuffed my belongings into my satchel. When the barge docked, I bid farewell to Captain Matteo.

He smiled and nodded. "*Fortuna*, Beppo," he said. Good luck.

One day until the wedding.

I went directly to Casa Madama, the home of Cardinal del Monte. A footman opened the door. I asked for the Cardinal.

"His Eminence is not here."

"Did he receive my letter?"

"Yes. But he is at the *serenade* for Tomasonni and Signorina Fiammini, at the Duke of Parma's palazzo."

"Serenade?"

"The celebration on the night before the wedding," the footman explained.

The Palazzo Farnese was only a few blocks away. Light spilled out from an open balcony onto a cluster of men singing in the piazza. Tomassoni was among them, unmistakable in his yellow doublet, sitting at a heavy table and drinking with his groomsmen.

I skirted through the shadows to the rear of the building, and dropped my satchel in a dark corner. Servants called back and forth to one another from within. I slipped into the kitchen, picked up a tray of wine-filled goblets and went upstairs, following a servant who was carrying a dish of pastries. Women's laughter reverberated in the large room. Dozens of women, all beautifully dressed, were chatting, laughing and leaning over the balcony railings to blow kisses to the young men serenading them below. Dolcetta was surrounded by a group of girls. I manoeuvred my way toward her.

"Wine, my lady?" I asked, handing her a glass. "Imported from Malta."

Startled, the bride-to-be looked up and bathed me in a dazzling smile. "Delighted," she replied, swiftly regaining her composure.

The other women also took glasses, emptying my tray.

"Dolcetta!"

I should have known that Fortunata would be close by.

My beloved set down her wine glass and crossed the room.

"Mother," she called. "You really must try these pastries!"

I quickly stepped onto the balcony to avoid detection.

Dolcetta reappeared in a few minutes. "Thank heaven you've come! Do you have a plan? Tell me quickly, my love. I can't divert my mother's attention for long."

"Garzone, so glad you could come to our party!" The speaker's malice belied his words.

I turned.

Giovan Tomassoni stood before me, smiling like a jackal, his sword drawn.

Chapter Nineteen: The Tipping Point

S'i' fossi foco, arderei lo mondo;
S'i' fossi vento, lo tempesterei ...

If I were fire, I'd burn the world away;
If I were wind, I'd turn my storms thereon ...

~Cecco Angiolieri

Tomassoni helped himself to Dolcetta's glass of wine and quickly downed its contents. "It is a tradition for a bride and groom to smash a glass and count the shards. The number of pieces represents the number of years of wedded bliss they can expect." He turned to Dolcetta and smiled. "Shall I perform the honour, my dear?"

Dolcetta stood frozen.

Tomassoni raised his glass and smashed it on my head, shattering it.

Bleeding and enraged, I slammed the empty tray against his shoulder. As he staggered backward, I twisted the pommel of his rapier out of his hand. He drew his dagger from his belt, but backed away from the blade that I now pointed toward him.

Fortunata rushed into the room.

"A sword!" yelled Tomassoni.

One of his comrades was quick to oblige.

All the guests flattened themselves against the walls as the groom and I faced each other.

"Stand aside, you villain! She doesn't love you," I barked.

Tomassoni sneered. He swiped at me with his friend's steel, but I evaded it and lunged at his exposed shoulder.

He parried, and lifted my sword with his own.

I leaped back again, narrowly avoiding the slash of his dagger with his other hand.

He sniggered. "Young and stupid! I've come for a wedding, but you've come for your own funeral!"

I dropped my left hand and snatched a cloth from a nearby table, sending a shower of empty wine glasses crashing to the floor. I whipped the cloth in circles around my arm to conceal my flank, waiting for an opportunity to thrust.

He sprang, knocked my sword away, and slammed his rapier against my wrapped arm.

Agony. My knees buckled, sending me to the floor. I grabbed the glass shards nearest to me and hurled them at him.

He slashed at my legs, but I succeeded in rolling away. I reached for my fallen sword and rose to confront him once again.

My grip felt wet. *Blood.*

Tomassoni brandished his sword in my face. "Caravaggio

neglected to teach you the first rule of swordsmanship: kill your opponent."

As he thrust at me, I dropped my tip and let the blade of my weapon slide against his until the *forte* deflected his sword. I twisted my wrist into *quarta*.

Somehow, my sword found purchase below his collarbone. He winced as the tip pierced his skin. "Yield!" I shouted. "Or die!"

Fortunata gasped. "Stop! Don't!"

"I'm no murderer," I responded. "Not yet. Giovan, tell them who killed Constantino."

Cardinal del Monte and the Duke of Parma charged into the room. "What is the meaning of this?" the Duke roared. "Guards!"

"Tell them!" I screamed at Tomassoni, pressing my point further into his flesh. "Tell them *now*, if you want to live!"

"Ranuccio killed Constantino," Tomassoni conceded. He dropped his sword.

"Say it again, louder!" I demanded.

Several guards entered the room, but the Duke raised his hand to halt them.

Tomassoni spat. "Ranuccio killed Constantino. This boy is innocent."

Del Monte whispered to the Duke, who nodded.

"All is well, Beppo," pronounced del Monte. "Lower your sword."

I stepped back.

"Beppo! You're hurt!" Dolcetta rushed toward me.

"It is not serious." I took her hand. "Marry me."

"Preposterous!" scoffed Tomassoni.

Again I raised my sword to his throat.

Fortunata glowered at me. "They are getting married tomorrow," she sputtered. "There is nothing you can do to stop it."

Incensed, I bellowed, "This is the man who attacked your carriage in Napoli!"

Tomassoni went white. "That was a mistake!" he protested. "We thought we were capturing a fugitive!"

"What?" Fortunata cried. "This is all—I don't—" She looked beseechingly at the Duke.

"Tell them you love me, Dolcetta," I implored.

"I do! Mother, I *do*! Yes, Beppo, I will marry you!"

This threw the crowd into an uproar.

"But the boy is penniless!" objected Fortunata, drawing her daughter close.

"These festivities have cost me a small fortune," the Duke muttered grimly. "The wedding will proceed as planned."

Lowering my sword, I bowed to the Duke. "Forgive me, Your Highness, but it would be a crime for Dolcetta to marry this man." I untied the purse at my belt and handed it to him. "Please accept this gift to compensate you for your expenses."

He opened the purse and spilled the coins into his hand. "Where did you get this gold? Did you steal it?"

Dolcetta slipped her hand into mine. Fortunata scowled.

I pulled General Colonna's letter from a pouch tucked at my waist and handed it to the Duke. "As you see from this letter, I now am wealthy in my own right. And I already am preparing to become a knight."

The Duke read the letter and handed it back to me.

"Indeed, this squire speaks the truth."

I bowed low before the astonished Fortunata. "Signora, I will provide for both you and your daughter in the manner you are accustomed to. I request that the wedding take place in three weeks' time. Cardinal del Monte, will you do the honours?"

"It will be my great pleasure," answered del Monte.

Fortunata took a deep breath and formally held out her hand for me to kiss.

Chapter Twenty: Present in Spirit

Per tuas semitas duc nos quo tendimus,
Ad lucem quam inhabitas.

By Thy ways, lead us where we are heading,
to the light Thou dwellest in.

~St. Thomas Aquinas, *Panis Angelicus*

At our marriage ceremony three weeks later, Dolcetta and I knelt in the sanctuary of the Church of San Luigi dei Francesi to receive communion from Cardinal del Monte. Wisps of incense curled around us as light streamed in through the arched windows. Young boys in white robes sang *Agnus Dei*.

We remained kneeling as our guests made their way to the altar and received communion: Fortunata and her titled acquaintances, Dolcetta's cousins and family friends, Don Marzio and General Colonna. The only person I had wanted to invite was Caravaggio. Of course, he couldn't risk being seen in Roma, but I felt that he was there in spirit. In the southwest corner of the church, nearest the sanctuary, his trio of *Matthews* graced three of the chapel's walls; one of the painted figures was Caravaggio's self-portrait.

As I knelt beside my darling bride, my head was filled with thoughts of the past year, most of them dark. The very events that had brought me to this moment also had caused me terrible anguish: Constantino lying in a pool of blood, Ranuccio's shocking fatal wound, the Vicar's screams as he was pushed overboard, Kheir Pasha's horrendous death. I did not want to be haunted by these memories; I wanted to bask in my present joy.

Del Monte touched my elbow. "You may kiss the bride."

I lifted her veil and kissed her soft mouth. Her hair smelled of lavender.

The Cardinal recited the benediction.

"*Et cum spiritu tuo*," the guests responded. And with your spirit.

We walked down the aisle, followed by the acolytes and the choir singing *Panis Angelicus*. As we gathered with our guests, I said earnestly to Cardinal del Monte, "Thank you for everything, Eccellenza."

"I am pleased to have been of assistance. I only wish I could have done more." He sighed and lifted his eyes to the stained glass window above us. I knew what he meant: he wished that he could have done more for Caravaggio. "But have no fear," he continued. "The winds may change yet." He smiled mysteriously, turning to Dolcetta. "Do you mean to leave soon for Malta?"

"Tomorrow, Eccellenza," she replied. "My mother will accompany us to Valletta." She turned to me with a radiant smile. "My brave knight, you've rescued me at last."

"No; it is you who have given me life."

She kissed me again.

Del Monte rocked back and forth impatiently on his heels.

"Perhaps we are both right," my bride decided. "Come. The reception awaits."

Outside, the guests had arranged themselves into two lines. We dutifully passed between them and were greeted by laughter and cheers, followed by showers of rice. I led Dolcetta out into the piazza, where we waved farewell to the crowd of well-wishers.

At the edge of the piazza, a man dressed all in black stood motionless. His cape was slung over one shoulder, half-concealing a sword. His broad-brimmed hat was pulled down low over his face.

"Signore!" I shouted, waving.

He put his finger to his lips, tipped his hat and bowed toward us. Then he rounded the corner of the church and disappeared into a waiting carriage. His black-gloved hand thrust through the curtains and formed a triumphant fist. The carriage pulled away in a cloud of dust.

Historical Note

Caravaggio is known for painting intense spiritual works with dramatic realism—but his lifestyle was a sharp contrast to the piety expressed in his works. He lived with abandon, picking fights in taverns and even killing a man in a sword fight. His circles of friends were wide and varied—from aristocrats to powerful clergymen to the most wretched of social outcasts. Like his canvasses—bright subjects set against dark backgrounds—his life was a study in extremes.

Caravaggio was born Michelangelo di Merisi in Milan in 1571. He grew up in the nearby town of Caravaggio—the name he adopted—among prominent members of the Colonna family. It was the Marchesa of Caravaggio who arranged for the young painter to apprentice in Milan with the artist Simone Peterzano. In 1592, Caravaggio moved to Rome to evade the consequences of having gravely wounded a policeman.

At first, Caravaggio was paid next to nothing to work for a man he called *Monsignore Salad,* since the employer fed him nothing but greens. The young artist spent years churning out hundreds of exquisite paintings of flowers and baskets of fruit. When Cardinal Francesco Maria Borbone del Monte discovered him in 1596, Caravaggio's life changed dramatically. With a patron to support him, he was free to develop his unique style. His celebrated artwork found its way into the family chapels and private galleries of Italy's social elite.

By 1606, when this novel begins, Caravaggio had become Italy's most famous painter. But he soon became its most infamous, after killing Ranuccio Tomassoni in a street brawl. Just as he had fled Milan, Caravaggio fled Rome. He spent the next five years in hiding, during which time he created what was to become his most famous work: *David with the Head of Goliath.* Caravaggio died in 1610—probably of lead poisoning—en route to Rome to receive a pardon from the Pope.

Unlike most established painters of his era, Caravaggio never formed a school, and never took an apprentice. In fact, he was so jealous of his own artistry that he was known to insult and even to attack those he believed had copied his style and methods.

He never signed his paintings—except for one: *The Beheading of John the Baptist,* which still hangs in St. John's Co-Cathedral on Malta.

By the late seventeenth century, Caravaggio's work had fallen into obscurity. It was not until the early 1930s—after the influential art critic Roberto Longhi championed his cause—that Caravaggio came back into the public eye. Since then, he has received the admiration he deserves as one of the preeminent artists of the Renaissance.

In the telling of this story, I draw upon several sources to create my portrayal of this controversial and most talented artist. I alter the chronology of some events in his life in order to construct a narrative. For example, Caravaggio did indeed slash one of his completed paintings, but that happened in Sicily, after my story ends. The dates and places of some of the paintings are matters of scholarly debate among art historians—but Caravaggio *did* kill Ranuccio Tomassoni and he *was* knighted on Malta. Following his escape from prison—which could only have been accomplished with some help—he was expelled from the Order of the Knights of St. John Hospitaller of Malta. I should add that Beppo is a purely fictional character.